DAMNATION

Julian Fane claims that some time ago he received an unsolicited typescript, to which was attached a note asking him to 'get it published or destroy it'. That typescript is now this book. Its narrator, Alan, relates that he was a clever boy from a humble home, whose scholarships and academic success led to his service at a Bletchley-style intelligence unit during the Second World War. He performs a kind act for the girl he loves and becomes entangled in political and ethical strings that threatens his love life and his career...

DAMNATION

DAMNATION

by

Julian Fane

Dales Large Print Books
Long Preston, North Yorkshire,
BD23 4ND, England.

British Library Cataloguing in Publication Data.

Fane, Julian
   Damnation.

   A catalogue record of this book is
   available from the British Library

   ISBN   1-84262-430-X pbk

First published in Great Britain 2004 by The Book Guild Ltd.

Published in Large Print 2006 by arrangement with
The Book Guild Ltd.

Dales Large Print is an imprint of Library Magna Books Ltd.

Printed and bound in Great Britain by
T.J. (International) Ltd., Cornwall, PL28 8RW

Contents

Introduction

Introductions are boring in my opinion, but this one is essential.

Some time ago I received a parcel of dog-eared typescript, together with a hand-written note that ran: 'PLEASE GET IT PUBLISHED OR DESTROY IT'. The post-mark on the brown wrapping paper was Hull.

The typescript, untampered with, is now on the point of publication. I believe it speaks for itself. Anyway, I have no more information to offer. Tracks seem to have been effectively covered by the author. To the best of my knowledge the factory town of Thornwick in the North of England does not exist.

Royalties, if or when earned by sales of the book, I expect only to repay the costs of production. If by chance the book should make money, no doubt somebody will come forward to claim it.

I have sanctioned the appearance of my name on the title page for better or for worse.

Julian Fane
Lewes, Sussex

In the Beginning

I am two persons in one – my sign of the zodiac is Gemini, the twins. My name is no longer the name with which I was baptised, and my home is no longer my native land. The book I hope to write will be the obituary of the other me, who will therefore, and perhaps, rest in peace.

I was born in 1921, the second and last child of parents who lived at 18 Gladstone Road, a terrace of houses in Thornwick. Father was called George, Mother Dorothy, my elder sister Ethel, and our cat Prince. We were poor and proud. The house we lived in, an artisan's dwelling, belonged to the Mill, the factory where Father worked – it was a 'tied cottage', our occupation of it was 'tied' to, and conditional upon, Father's employment. The two terraces on either side of Gladstone Road had been built by the family that owned the Mill, and all the householders were metal-workers, like Father.

He fought throughout the First World War and survived. He came home and found his pre-war job waiting for him. He put these pieces of luck down to the benevolence of his employer and the grace of God. He often said he never expected a third piece of luck, although accidents for better or worse are supposed to come in threes. But his God again smiled on him: Mother agreed to be his wife.

She was getting on for thirty, two years older than he was – nobody in our circumstances could afford to marry young. She was one of the teachers at the school for the children of the Mill employees. They must have been nice-looking, he black-haired with dark brown eyes, she tall and slim, and wearing her long fair hair in a bun. They were good people, and both cradle Catholics – the Roman Church was active in Thornwick.

My first memories were of Mother – in our walk of life how could it be different? We were together while Father worked long five-and-a-half-day weeks, and Ethel was at school. Sentimental details are too hackneyed to supply. I assumed that I was the apple of her eye, she could be sure that she was the apple of mine, and our relationship rested securely, if not permanently, on this basis. Father frightened me. He had a sceptical and cynical expression: things he had seen in the war, and suffered and maybe done, would have accounted for it. My best memory is of the soft palms of his hands – they were cushioned, neither dry nor horny, and, as I found out later, peculiar to certain first-rate manual workers.

Ethel meant pain for me from the word go. She pinched me when she could do so without discovery. I suppose she had reason to be jealous, she was a combination of our parents' worst features and traits – too heavy, too tall, too suspicious, too competitive. In addition, she was bad at her books.

Home had a smell which I loved when I was a child and hated ever afterwards. It smelt of cooking and washing, and the smelliness was concentrated by the limited interior space and the climate which discouraged the admission of fresh air for much of the year. The drying of clothes was more odoriferous than the washing: the old chair in front of the range seemed to have integral blue overalls draped over it, not to mention the personal items of a family of four.

Comfort of all kinds was restricted. Until I was five or six I slept in a home-made cot in my parents' bedroom, Ethel slept on the settee in our parlour, and Tim, the apprentice who worked with Father, lodged with us and occupied the spare upstairs room. Our bath and hot-water boiler were in a lean-to at the back of our house, and the lavatory was there too. In winter the only fairly warm room was the kitchen. We children were sometimes allowed to take a stone hot-water bottle to bed.

The books belonging to my parents were a Bible, a Missal, a few teaching texts and a copy of *Lorna Doone* by R.D. Blackmore. I was slow to learn to read. I shamed my mother, who would not send me to nursery school in case her failure to knock literacy into my head should be revealed. With the very best intentions she paved a road to hell for me with lessons. I hated to disappoint her, was horrified when I made her rant and even cry, and panic scattered my wits more effectively than the hieroglyphs on the printed page. Irritation on her side evoked rage on mine, or perhaps it was vice versa. Her questions were unanswerable: Why couldn't I? Why wouldn't I? Why was she saddled with the dunce of Thornwick? Punishment hardened both our hearts.

It was Ethel who came to our rescue, though whether or not I should be grateful to her is a moot point – the attempt to educate the proletariat has proved disastrous. My sister in one of our friendly chats spat the word 'Blindie' in my direction. It upset me; she liked that; and one day she advised our mother to spare her breath, not to bother about my ABC, because I was blind as well as thick. She was rebuked: nice girls did not say nasty things to their little brother. But Mother investigated, Father was consulted, our parish priest, Father Donnelly, was called in, and eventually my eyes were tested.

I was short-sighted.

Those two hyphenated words have an unfortunate bearing on the rest of my life.

My sight was corrected with spectacles – I was four or five years old. The outward effect was that I amused the grown-ups, whose previous reactions to me had been pity or exasperation. Instead of dropping things, tripping, losing people I was meant to be following, and failing to read notices such as 'Gentlemen' over the entrances to public lavatories, I uttered exclamations of wonder and delight that called forth laughter.

For example, I said I was glad to know where the tree trunks and drainpipes went. I thanked heaven that I was no longer hit on the nose by balls thrown for me to catch. I expressed my pleasure to be able to understand words like star, horizon, landscape and aeroplane.

Other outward effects were that I was suddenly quick to learn, and startled Mother so much as to cause her to shed more tears, now tears of relief. The sighs and head-shakings of yesteryear turned into compliments and kisses. Lessons were no longer an ordeal for either of us; they were fun and games, and competitions for prizes.

Soon my parents agreed that I would not bring shame on them at school.

Mother said: 'You'll be with Ethel there... Your sister will take you to school... You two will be together... And you'll be able to play with the other boys.'

Father said: 'You'll have no excuse now if you don't shine at school... You go and make us proud of you, son!'

They were dreadful psychologists – every sentence they chose plucked at my nerves. My dislike of Ethel was mutual. To be in her tender care alarmed me. I already sensed that I was not a good mixer – other boys could be bad news. And Father's encouragement took the form of threats.

My fears were not misplaced. Ethel considered me as much of a burden as I considered her a menace. I happened to be the only boy of my age at school who wore glasses, and my classmates stole them, tried them on their noses, tickled me when I could not see them, called me Goggles, and made me miserable.

On the other hand – or was it the same hand? – I had an extra incentive to do better than they did at work. But of course they sought revenge for having had to wear the dunce's hat on my account.

These experiences were the downside of the discovery of my faulty eyesight. It had an upside. It revolutionised my mentality and psyche.

I began to read as people should read, for pleasure, in order to be delighted. I rushed through our baby books, and gravitated via the Bible and the Missal to *Lorna Doone.* The story of that book was hackneyed before it was written, and since then has been retold, filmed, televised, innumerable times. In my seventh or eighth year, not knowing it was corny, I was thrilled by the immense strength of John Ridd, loved his heroism and honesty, and dreaded the Doones apart from Laura. On another level I suppose it satisfied my childish morality to be assured that the right side could prevail against its enemies.

Further reasons probably explain why reading meant so much to me. First, considering my sign of the zodiac, a book was my getaway into another set of circumstances and another life. By leaving reality behind and absorbing myself in printed matter, I gratified some mysterious innate urge.

Secondly, reading was soon mixed up with religion. I drew near to a God scarcely distinguishable from the dominant figure of John Ridd. The Garden of Eden was in the West Country, and the Devil was a Doone.

My parents were pious. The only guest ever invited into our house was Father Donnelly: he came to lunch on one Sunday per year and almost ate us into penury. The religious teaching that was dinned into me by Mother, then at Bible Class, put a name to all the consequences of the recognition of my short-sightedness. God, not Ethel, had come to my rescue and introduced me into the charmed circle of bookworms. A miracle had occurred: I was the stuff, the person, over whom God had deigned to wave His miraculous wand – I was the empty vessel He had filled.

My imagination ran away with me. If my childhood was mildly depressive, my early youth was manic. I felt that God was protecting me even when Ethel was in punitive mood or I was getting the worst of it in the playground at school. I prayed excessively, put too many eggs in the basket of God, picked no holes in the logic or illogic of the Christian faith, and stopped my ears in principle to the blaspheming of my contemporaries.

Regrets are for stupid people. My parents paid no attention to my overwrought state – they were pleased that I kept on improving my prospects. They might have saved themselves heartache in the future if they had somehow stepped on the brakes.

To hell with the do-gooders! I now read the English newspapers masochistically, and have registered that do-gooders attribute my failings to the hardships of my youth. They are wrong, as usual.

Do-gooders should shut their mouths and hang their heads with shame, for they bear a large part of responsibility for the catastrophes of my lifetime. They helped the Bolsheviks to seize power and wreck Russia. They gave Hitler his chance to wage war on the world and on Jewry in particular. They are the liberals who have ushered in the worst governments and the terrible dictatorships of the left.

I know that do-gooders like to mingle with peasants and underdogs, but wonder if any of them know how boys like me are brought up. Perhaps some boys of my type are pleased to be admired for their conquest of pauperism and deprivation. I write for myself: I was deprived of nothing after my sight was restored. No prince of the blood was more cossetted than I was. I had every comfort, and an extended court of persons devoted to my well-being and the promotion of my interests.

For I was clever. My green-eyed enemies were in a minority at Thornwick. The majority included my family, its friends, other parents of bright boys, and school-teachers, and local authorities, and educational bodies from farther afield. I was the star turn, the good example, the ray of hope, the proof that pie was not always in the sky.

Practically, at home, I was moved into Tim's room, while Tim now had to sleep on the floor of the passage to the bathroom: my own night's rest took precedence over part of the rent our lodger had paid. Our parlour was reserved for my homework and studies – Ethel did not get into it until I got out. Special food was bought and cooked for me if I did not fancy what the others were eating. I was deferred to by everybody in every way, so that I would learn more and learn it quicker, rise above my breeding and bestow status on my relations.

Conversations with my parents at such times come back to me. Mother would warm my bed and, when I had collapsed into it, bring me Ovaltine or Benger's Food to strengthen me.

'You have a good long sleep, Alan, then you'll do even better tomorrow,' she was apt to say.

Sometimes I complained that my head was spinning round – I had mild attacks of vertigo after overworking.

'Does your head spin, Mother?'

'I haven't so much to spin with in my head as you have in yours. What a joy you are to me, Alan! You're a dream of mine come true. Scholarship's a wonderful thing! I'm proud of you already, and have reason to believe I'll be prouder one day.'

Father put pressure on me, too.

He was concerned when I was indisposed, and expressed hopes that I was not going to disappoint Mother.

He was apt to say: 'You've done me a favour at work, son – they reckon more for me because you're bound to be "white-collar" instead of "blue". You've let a little light in our lives, you and your jumping ahead of all the other boys round here.'

My religion was yet another spur not to waste time in rest or recuperation. I left my bed for God's sake as well as to please generally. The whole family was additionally religious because of my achievements: there was reflected glory to thank for, which might have widespread and worthwhile side-effects.

First Communion raised me on to a peak, where I was closer to God than ever before. It happened in winter, in wintry weather – snow was on the ground and the silver brightness of the sun was not warm enough to melt it. I wore a new suit of clothes with long trousers – clothes new to me though old to the previous owner. I remember the sleeves covered my hands, allowing for future growth, and that I was worried by my down-at-heel shoes. As we trooped out of church Father Donnelly patted me on the back and said to my parents: 'This lad has far to go, God willing.' I was flattered, and saw my way ahead in mystical terms. Whether or not I confessed my ambitions to be a priest or a saint to any other mortal escapes my memory. For all I know, my parents might have foreseen a dog collar round my neck: they were more churchy than ever on account of their great blessing, me.

Disillusionment was waiting in the wings: what goes up must come down. Our parlour was cold in winter, and when I worked there a fire was laid and lit in the grate. One week-end day I set to work early, continued until late, and was worried by the amount of coal burned in order to keep me from congealing. I mentioned my worry to Mother, referring to the expense – unselfishness was part of the high tone in force at 18 Gladstone Road.

She said: 'Your father gets the coal at the Mill.'

'Oh, I see.' But I persisted. 'Is it free?'

'Well – he only brings a lump or two home at a time.'

'Does anyone know?'

'Ask no questions and you'll be told no lies. And don't go gossiping, Alan. We wouldn't want to be thought at fault.'

I was shocked temporarily. But I held my tongue: the moral dilemma defeated me – Father was pinching the coal, but only for admirable motives, to keep me warm and well, and he had not been caught.

The worst thing about my upbringing was that I lived in a road named after a liberal. Seriously, I was not scarred by the lowliness of my birth, and I rebut the imputation that my parents were slave drivers and pushed and pulled me inexorably in the direction I was later to take. The period between the correction of my eyesight and my first big examination was comfortable in the extreme, and I repudiate the excuses made for me in do-gooding quarters where crime and sin are taboo words.

The examination in question was intended to sift out potential scholars, suitable for admission to the Grammar School in the county town. I spent three nights with my aunt, my father's sister, who was a dressmaker and lived there, and two days, from eight o'clock until noon and from two till four, scribbling in a church hall. I had no noticeable nerves in those days, and not much difficulty with the papers; but another examinee vexed me.

He was called Hendrix, William Hendrix, although I did not know his first name until later. He must have been thirteen or fourteen when I was about eleven. In the morning of the first day of the exam, as I stood in a queue waiting for the hall to open up, the boy standing behind me drew my attention to Hendrix.

'He'll do best,' the boy said, pointing.

Hendrix was already as tall as a man, and good-looking. He had wavy golden hair and pink cheeks, and laughed a lot. He was also different from most of the boys, who were silent and apprehensive.

The opinion, the assumption, of my neighbour, jarred. I was accustomed not only to thinking that I would win top marks, but also to others thinking it. Competition in the raw was a strange idea, and the possibility of not being top dog unpleasant.

'Why do you say that?' I asked.

'He's in our school. He's brilliant, and awfully good at games.'

'What's he called?'

'Hendrix. He's half-Dutch or something. He'll soon be out of sight.'

'What do you mean?'

'He'll be ahead of the rest of us. He's planning to buy a Rolls-Royce.'

'What's that?'

'Golly! Where do you come from? It's a car that costs big money.'

'But he won't be able to drive for years.'

'He's going to earn enough money to buy a Rolls between now and when he can drive it. You wait and see – you'll be seeing him in his Roller!'

I suspended judgment. At least I hope I did. But in our mid-morning break he approached me, smiled down at me with his easy open smile, and said: 'They tell me you're the opposition.'

I asked him to explain.

'You're supposed to have a head on your shoulders. Is that true?'

I was nonplussed – people at Thornwick did not go in for banter.

'Oh well,' he said, 'this is chicken feed – wait till we're battling it out for honours degrees!' And he turned his back on me and swung away to chat and laugh with better company.

I hated him then for his charm and sophistication, and tried to understand his cryptic remarks and felt I had made a fool of myself.

Positively, I hoped to have another chance to gain his favour with my wit and knowledge. But in further breaks between papers and for dinner – our word for their lunch – he was otherwise occupied, joking with cronies and playing French and English in a yard behind the church hall.

The less notice he took of me the harder I tried to excel in the exam. There were no more than twenty of us sitting, so the supervisors were able to correct our papers in the evenings and, early on the third day, announce the results. I was the winner, but had only beaten Hendrix by one mark. It was a less comprehensive victory than I had aimed for – in fact, as he was not slow to point out, nearly a defeat.

He strode over with hand outstretched, exuding ten times the confidence of his conqueror, and laughed in my face and said: 'You won by a whisker. You've lived up to your reputation. But count no chickens – I'll get my own back. I never fail to get my own back.'

I was again bemused by his personality, and somewhat stunned by his genial threat. But I recovered – the satisfaction of my aunt and my parents was infectious. It became clear to all of us that a transformation scene was in progress – I was no longer a poor working-class boy from nowhere, but somebody on whom prizes, bursaries and financial encouragement were being showered, who was waving goodbye to Gladstone Road and knocking on the door of a better address, and beyond that bound for the Groves of Academe.

My family did not repine. My parents saw

that their ambition was being fulfilled, not that they were losing a son. The general excitement excited me. One day or night I seemed to be enlightened by the thought that my intellect was invincible, and nobody, none of the Hendrixes who might cross my path, would ever stop me getting whatever I wanted.

I am not swanking. I am recording a conviction and a sensation, the experience of which was a tremendous privilege. And by means of this autobiographical ego-trip, I am trying to trace the source of my mistakes.

Good Intentions

I worked hard in the years leading to war in 1939, and was successful – within limits.

My work was exclusive of other interests. I studied in schools more or less far from Thornwick, and lodged with relations or the friends of relations as a rule. Home was wherever my teachers and my books were. Admittedly there were terms and there were holidays; but in the holidays I had courses to attend, or was in receipt of free tuition, or had been set homework with which I needed help not available in the vicinity of Gladstone Road. My parents did not reproach me for neglecting them. They were too honest to complain of their wishes coming true. Perhaps they recognised, as I did, that we no longer had much in common.

Socially I was a flop. My acquaintances never turned into friends. I myself was at least as standoffish as my schoolmates seemed to be. Luckily my path did not cross again with Hendrix's; but he had infected me with the bug of competitiveness. To beat other boys in my way, to beat the opposition, was now more my spur than idealism, or a vocation, or a desire to please my parents. In the context of friendliness, because of the above, I was reluctant to associate with my peers, who might pick my brains and steal a march on me.

At the same time I could hardly lower myself so far as to pal up with the morons. The middling solution of the problem was that I agreed to become the backroom boy for the fast set – I told idlers how to write their essays and pass their tests. I was useful to them also for being the butt of their humour. They called me Potty because I was a pot-hunter, a winner of prizes, and were amused by my being so unfunny. They were all large, muscular, sporting and patronising: they laughed at my appearance and Yorkshire accent, and lifted me on to the top of cupboards, and made a joke of my merry quips which were not forthcoming. I did not like it, but supposed it was better than nothing.

Sex deigned to leave me be while I concentrated on higher or lower things – bookwork, that is. Broad talk and smut were a foreign language so far as I was concerned; and I was unaware of sexual action while I was at boys' day-schools. The facts of life had been explained to me by Ethel, but first I thought she was teasing, then regarded the sordid truth as irrelevant.

What a shock to the system when manhood struck me amidships!

Like reading, like finding I was not stupid, it was a revolution. I was sixteen years of age, and the past was put in a brand new perspective. I ceased to be only a swot. I grew physically, was proud of my male voice and other physical facilities, downgraded intellect, took a second look at girls, and prepared to reorder priorities.

A rare bird – a schoolmaster with talent, not a girl – had drawn my attention to the Spanish Civil War. As a result I began to appreciate that beyond the good and evil of my religious background were political Right and Left. For the first time I also heard of two other antonyms – or were they somehow synonymous? – Marxism and Nazism.

The same schoolmaster gave me personal advice which was influential.

He said: 'We're going to war. Your cronies do you no credit. The giggling's got to stop. Consider your future and where you stand about fighting and killing your fellows, and which of them you want to fight and kill! Life's about to become more difficult for everyone. You're a Catholic, aren't you? Better tell your God to do us all a good turn for a change and without delay!'

Round about the time in question I returned to Thornwick.

Ethel reproached me for coming home so seldom. She touched a sore spot and provoked me into saying I had better things to do.

'Oh you have, have you?' she batted back. 'Hark at him! You've had the best of us here, and now you turn your nose up. Well, I'm telling you, when you're laying wounded in the trenches you'll be sorry. You think you're important, but you're nothing but a selfish pig in my opinion and always were.'

'And you're a reactionary,' I returned, resorting to a vocabulary of which I scarcely knew the meaning.

At some stage of my visit I asked Mother what her politics were.

'Oh I don't like politics,' she replied.

'You mustn't say that,' I scolded her. 'This war will be all to do with politics. We've got to know what we're fighting for and against.'

'You'll have to talk to your father, Alan. I can't bear to think of another war, and you in the army.'

'Who says I'll be in the army? Don't worry!'

I dished out cold comfort, and did as I was told.

Father answered my question thus: 'Sometimes I vote one way and sometimes another. Makes no difference – all politicians want is their way and my money.'

'But this war, what do you think of that?'

'Not a lot.'

'Should I keep out of it?'

'How do you mean?'

'I could be a conscientious objector.'

'Oh no, son, no – "conchies" were dregs in the last war.'

'I know you were a soldier, but–'

'Shut the buts, lad! Do your duty and say your prayers, and you won't go far wrong.

Maybe your eyesight will preserve you.'

'Do you know about communism, Father?'

'I know it's silly talk. The working class always gets it in the neck in the long run.'

'Modern communism's different.'

'Is it now?'

'Communism's as against the Nazis as we are.'

'Who says so? You can't trust Bolshies.'

'You're completely wrong, Father.'

'We'll see.'

The main upshot of these conversations was that I renounced my religion.

I had no faith that God would prevent the war; was not in tune with Mother's escapism; and considered Father ignorant and old-fashioned.

My argument was, consciously or unconsciously, that if Father could believe in a Catholic God and Goddess and heaven and hell, why should I not believe in the incredible too – in the possibility of a just world and a heaven on earth man-made by atheists?

The latter question was posed – no more than posed. I was uncommitted, I always was a floating voter: that was the strangest thing.

War broke out, and my poor sight compensated for every difficulty it had caused me. I was rejected by the armed services, and moved from my final school into the Ministry of Defence, and thence to various hush-hush departments staffed by boffins.

To start with I probably fought as safe and pleasant a war as was available. In the vernacular of the time, my billet was cushy, not half. I lived in a manor house in a village in the depths of the countryside, worked where I slept, ate in, and wore civvies. There was a town within bicycling distance, where we watched films, could dance on Saturday nights, and swim in summer.

There were twenty-five of us approximately. We were not like Bletchley – we called Bletchley 'the beehive' – our common denominator was nonconformity. In the beginning we thought we resembled a monastery, since no women were included, but afterwards we compared ourselves with members of a secret society. Secrecy was definitely the name of our game, though not just for the obvious reason that our work might be useful to the enemy.

Each was a specialist in one exclusive field. We had a physicist, a metallurgist, a chemist, a marine biologist, an engineer, a geographer, experts on flight, deserts, the poles, diverse aspects of science; and each man's work was not understood by the other men. We might discuss a line of inquiry with our Director of Studies, but then had to produce a theoretical paper that would be despatched to a committee of people elsewhere capable of evaluating the research and its practical possibilities.

The work was pressurised – we wished not to lose the war – and frustrating: often our labours were unacknowledged by anybody. My own experience was typical: only once in four years was an idea of mine taken beyond the pen and paper stage. The idea was a cybernetic formula – it would mean nothing to ninety-nine point nine percent of potential readers of this book, and is beside the point.

I made a friend at our Camp X. He was the physicist – and I shall call him Arthur. Arthur was childlike in stature and in his purity of spirit; but he had the full ration of manly and irrepressible hair that seems to grow out of the scalps of the intelligentsia. Oddly enough, although I was often compared to Johnny-head-in-air, the basis of our friendship was that he tried in vain to interest me in physics, and I tried to teach him how to ride a bike, travel by bus, buy the right things to drink in a pub, and suffer fools more gladly than he was inclined to.

Sex was a problem for most of us, if not all – big brains are not necessarily a guide to the size of carnal appetites. Some men were married and missing wives, others missed affection of any old sort. Flirtations with the household staff led to complications. Sex with villagers was a recipe for disaster, pick-ups in town were tricky, and every sexual scene was regarded as the setting for the crime of treason.

Solutions were provided gradually. More holidays were sanctioned. Several wives moved house to be near husbands. Our appointments were pretty well for the duration – the powers-that-were did not want to let us loose amongst German spies; but gaps appeared in our ranks, and were sometimes filled by women. Chivalry cannot conceal the fact that our female colleagues were visually a disappointment: if they merited a place at our table, they were almost by definition not made to supply our demands. Pudding-basin haircuts and no time for the acts of dalliance were not quite what was pined for. But exceptions crept in under unlikely disguises, for instance a pretty girl who designed booby traps, and then Carol, a dietician.

She was twenty-two when I was nineteen.

She was blonde, small, healthy, lively. She had an obstinate set of chin, but her figure compensated for any faults that could be found with her face. It was seductive, it had that indescribable quality which can never be acquired – her clothes, instead of covering up her body, revealed it and tantalised.

Carol stirred senses I had not known I possessed. Arthur was surprised that I should allow myself to be distracted by her proximity. When I described my feelings, he asked me why I did not declare myself without delay.

'Because she wouldn't look at me, she wouldn't listen.'

'But I've seen her looking at you, I've seen you talking to her.'

'You don't understand. She's out of reach. I've never met a girl like Carol before.'

'Well, sex is only a want, it's not a need.'

'That's logic, and man doesn't live by logic alone.'

I suppose I cast sheep's eyes at her from behind my specs, for she played up and pretended to flirt for a laugh. She called me Romeo and Gorgeous, and made kissing noises when we passed each other in passages. She mocked Arthur and me at the same time – we were her 'he-men'.

Occasionally, for instance in the village pub where we all congregated, I did manage to have a word or two with her.

Once she asked me: 'What do you do, or can't you tell me?'

'No,' I replied, meaning that I could and would tell her. But as soon as I started she interrupted me: 'Don't say another word for pity's sake – *parlez-vous Anglais*, by any chance?'

Another time she said rather accusingly, 'I bet you love your Mummy.' When I replied, 'I do, but not too much,' she said by way of a grudging apology, 'Sorry – I thought you might be a diddums.'

She really was saucy – and no wonder, since she was fawned on by enough men to play cricket against one another. She was soon the spoilt darling, and was apt to imbibe an excess of libations from her votaries in the pub.

One evening in summer she allowed me to escort her back to Camp X. My colleagues had left the pub earlier – there was a visitation from on high scheduled for the following day – and I had hung back in case Carol should condescend to notice me. She did, she was slightly tipsy, and she asked for an arm to keep her on the straight and narrow.

It was late, dusky, and a moon shone down on our walk along the empty road.

'A moon, how romantic!' she said.

And in a less giggly way she said: 'A lovely night, a night for love, don't you think?'

I agreed verbally.

She inquired: 'Have you got a girlfriend?'

I mumbled an ambiguous negative.

'Or a boyfriend?'

'No.'

'Would you like to have a girlfriend?'

'Yes, very much.'

'I'm your girl for tonight.'

'Are you?'

'Of course. And you're the only boy in the world.'

We laughed at the quotation from the popular song.

'Have you had anything to do with a woman, Alan?'

'Not really.'

'Do you know what love is?'

'Yes, sort of.'

'Come here!'

She kissed me. She taught me to kiss back. We stood in the roadway, kissing and kissing.

Then she said: 'That's lesson one. "Home, James!"'

'Oh Carol!'

I wished to detain her.

'Listen,' she said. 'Can't you hear "lights out"?' She was referring to the military bugle call. 'We've got to win the war tomorrow.'

'I love you,' I said.

She laughed more at me than with me, and called me funny.

We reached Camp X and she gave me a different kind of kiss good night – it was like a butterfly's wing touching my lips.

'Be sure to wipe the lipstick off,' she said.

In the morning, the party of bigwigs arrived to cheer us up and on, and to inspect and investigate us. A member of that party was a tall handsome golden-haired man of about my age. We recognised each other, and he greeted me jovially and told me he had been posted to Camp X – we would be buddies.

He was Hendrix.

In wartime life accelerates.

I cannot remember dates, dates are not significant, and the water that once flowed and flooded under the bridge now swirls in distant seas.

Hendrix did not arrive at Camp X in a Rolls-Royce, which was a relief. On the other hand, he did not need a Rolls-Royce in order to prove that he was already a well-heeled man of the world. He had become an aeronautical engineer, married and fathered a child. He had worked in industry for a year or so before the war, he had earned good money – he was steps ahead of the rest of us. He had not been called into the armed services: a malicious rumour suggested that he was passed unfit because he had hammer toes, but I think his potential help with the war effort spared him. He must have been good at his work. Socially, at Camp X, he was a controversial figure, a breath of fresh air to some, a loudmouth and charlatan to others.

He was overpoweringly friendly to me. I was to call him Bill. We were to be sounding boards for each other's bright ideas. And we were to meet and chew the rag out of office hours. He had bought a house in the vicinity – two cottages knocked together, quite extensive, and picturesque to boot – and insisted on my bicycling over for Sunday lunches. He invited several of us – where did he get the food? His wife Maureen was that unusual combination, pretty and earthy – she looked vague, but, despite food rationing, vaguely fed parties of adults and her vaguely well brought-up little boy, Winston.

They were one of those perfect twosomes

that make singles grind their teeth. He was Aryan enough to melt the heart of Hitler, an old-style British type, outgoing, capable of winning a match and writing a sonnet, an intellectual without side, an all-rounder and a regular chap. Maureen was an ideal match for a man of Bill's stamp, too feminine to show how efficient she was, attractive in an impersonal way.

I could not swallow them. I could not resist them. No doubt I was jealous, and no doubt I wanted to see what he was up to.

As I remember, I twigged immediately that Bill and Carol were in love. But surely I first realised that Carol did not love me. Innocent as I was, there was no mistaking her embarrassment and hostility when I sued for more kisses or at least for some of her sweet talk in the moonlight. I asked her if she was going to the pub on such-and-such a night: she said no, she did not know, she did not want to be pinned down, she might, if so she would bicycle by herself. I asked what I had done wrong: she said oh, why did I have to ask stupid questions, and would I please desist? I asked for time alone with her, so that I could find out where I stood: she said no hope of that, she was far too busy, and where I had to stand was on my own two feet.

From knowing who was not loved, to knowing who was, took no major effort of perception. Perhaps I should remind readers of the permissive and immoral generations that adultery was a deadly secret in the 1940s. Bill Hendrix and Carol showed me they were lovers by means of their discretion. They scarcely spoke to each other in public. She steered clear of the pub more often than not, and never drank much. He and she were sometimes missing for a longer or shorter period. And her eyes shone ever brighter, and her lips looked wickedly kissable.

I kept mum. I would have felt worse if I had sneaked on them. I was very cut up and thought of asking for a transfer to another place of work.

But the German invasion of Russia shook the kaleidoscope of war, and the gallant gloom prevalent since the outbreak was translated into a more positive pattern.

At Camp X politics had not been a favourite topic of conversation. Nobody wanted to rock the boat we were all in. Nobody was sure that we had a political future. Victory, however far over the horizon it might be, the possibility of victory, had the effect of fire-water on politically-minded Red Indians. No one was a Nazi any more, although admirers of Hitler and Mussolini had been numerous pre-war; but at last the worshippers of Karl Marx and the Russian Bolsheviks, the members of the Communist Party, the socialists, the liberals and the malcontents, were granted the freedom to dance round their golden calf.

Arthur and I, a couple scorned for their lack of commitment, had heard tell of the horrors of the USSR and the yearnings of the Russian masses for the good old auto-cratic days. But the communists at Camp X, boffins and penpushers, emerged from their shells slavering for more oppression and extra buckets of blood. They had the turn of events on their side – Russia was our ally, and everything was allowable that rendered comfort and support to Uncle Joe Stalin and his *moujiks,* beginning with hand-knitted socks and ending with the liqui-dation of the English aristocracy, middle class, conservatives, independent spirits and slackers.

The atmosphere at Camp X deteriorated into a microcosmic version of the traditional strife and backbiting amongst the Groves of Academe. I can be satirical about it now, now we can all see that the views of the communists of yesteryear and their fellow-travellers were blinkered and partisan, but at the time I floated leftwards. I wanted the USSR to win the war for us; I knew too little of its internal governance and too much of the failings of our own, and could always see that Marxism made some sense on paper. Besides, I confess without pride, the communists I associated with were bigger bullies than the so-called reactionaries, who peddled the status quo and laws tested by time.

My sympathies were reinforced by two other influences. The USSR was temporarily getting beaten, and underdogs do have charm. Secondly, at the Hendrix house, I was relieved to get away from Carol and communism, quite amused by the company that assembled there, somehow hypnotised by my rival, and enjoyed Maureen's cooking.

Bill Hendrix had studied at Y University, located nearby, and invited foreign exchange graduates to his lunches and dinners. He also entertained captains of the industry which had employed him, and I grant he was an excellent host and controlled the conversation of his guests with tact. In his cottage I heard good and calm expositions of the advantages and disadvantages of a free market economy versus the abolition of the profit motive.

I listened and was swayed, but would recollect in the nick of time, before I had signed on any dotted line, that I was dead against the establishment of a classless society, which would check my rise into the altitudinous regions of my ambitions. I did my best to remember that Lenin and Stalin ruled by terror and murder as I chatted with Russian visitors to University Y in the cosy ambiance created by Bill and Maureen.

I made the acquaintance of a number of foreign scholars, European refugees who hailed from the USA or Canada, also Swedes and Africans. University Y seemed to have a flourishing line in postgraduate studies in a variety of subjects. In the Hendrixes' house I struck up circumstantial friendships with an African Professor of the History of Slavery, a Swedish student of nursery rhymes, and two Russians from Portugal who were diplomats as well as the authors of learned studies of the links between languages.

And I must admit we all had fun together for one reason or another. The lunches were long and the dinners late, wine was as plentiful as the food, and probably everybody enjoyed such celebratory occasions the more because they were rare – for at least a year they had been non-existent. Bill's rosy cheeks and fulfilled countenance backed up his hospitable skills and ringing laughter, and Maureen betrayed no sign of unease.

Then Bill received a summons from government quarters to leave Camp X in a hurry and carry on his work elsewhere.

The hinge of fate opens and closes with the rapidity of a rat trap.

Think of love at first sight, a marriage dependent on words of two or three letters, a baby created in a matter of minutes! A sentence can make or break a career, a photograph or accident or bullet or bomb define destinies, a politician's signature declare war, the whim of a bacillus cause an epidemic.

Fate acted in character at Camp X.

Naturally, loving Carol, my hopes were revitalised by the prospect of the elimination of the man who also loved her and, unlike me, was loved in return.

The fact that her hopes, if any, were disappointed, or at least that her happiness was rudely interrupted, she took on her stubborn little chin. Apart from looking rather ill, she showed no sign of cardiac pain. Regrets were voiced in respect of Bill's departure, but once I heard her remark with a shrug of her shoulders that he was right to go to a bigger and better job.

When he had gone, I tried again to see her alone. I asked if she would like a walk on a nice day. I invited her to the pub one evening. She refused. But I was encouraged that she did so politely, as if with a touch of sorrow.

She fell ill, submitted to an indisposition of some kind and stayed in her bedroom. Meals were carried up to her by the kitchen staff, although apparently she had no appetite.

While I worried about her and wondered, Bill Hendrix turned up. He had said his goodbyes to Camp X, so I was surprised to notice his car, his modest car – a Hillman, I think it was – in our car park at five o'clock one evening. He must be with Carol, I deduced sourly.

At about five-thirty he barged into my bed-sitting-room and said without preamble: 'We've got to talk.' He shut the door behind him, slumped down on my second chair, covered his eyes with one hand, and confessed: 'I'm in deep trouble.'

I had not invited him in. He had not knocked. My colleagues as a rule refrained from theatrical entrances and melodramatic confessions. And I did not have to jump far to conclude that his trouble was love and Carol was involved or responsible.

Bill began again.

'I'm sorry – I've no time – and I believe I can trust you – our friend's pregnant.'

'Oh,' said I.

'I'd marry her if I could but I can't. Her people are Scottish Protestants, and she's their only child. There's no hope at home – and she won't consider an abortion.'

I refrained from pointing out that she, not he, was the one in trouble, and asked: 'Why are you telling me?'

'You're fond of her, aren't you?'

'I was.'

'Listen, whatever you do or don't do is your business, but I wanted you to know that Carol and I are finished for ever. Maureen's my number one priority – I shouldn't have strayed – and Carol feels the same.'

'Carol doesn't like me.'

'Not true!'

'Anyhow, I couldn't marry her, I couldn't afford to financially – and I haven't got any more time than you have.'

'Oh God!'

'Hard lines on Carol!'

'Please go and see her. She'd like that, she said so. Don't worry about money – money's not the problem. Don't think too badly of me!'

He stood up and left without another word.

Twenty-four hours of inner turmoil and indecision later, I knocked on her bedroom door, spoke my name, and was told to wait.

At length she opened the door and faced me, fully dressed, head held high, smiling. Slowly, a tear or two rolled out of her blue eyes and down her cheeks, which had been so pink and cheerful.

I patted her. I offered her my shoulder. I hugged her better. She was apologetic and grateful. Friendship was re-established over the next days. I loved her again, but we were both shy, and our private hopes and fears were hidden.

Meanwhile another strange situation developed. I received an invitation from one of the two Russians who were on an exchange visit at University Y from their Portuguese university base. At the Hendrix house they were known as Clem and Vlad – I never discovered their real names, and I seem to remember that the tall bag of bones was called Vlad for a joke, after the Hungarian despot Vlad the Impaler. It was Clem who rang to ask me out to tea at a café in a nearby village – Clem was rotund and jolly.

I accepted. It was an outing, a treat not to

be missed. But the café was for truck drivers, a grubby place, and tea came in mugs with slices of toast and marge. On the other hand Clem and Vlad spoke good English, were amusing, also complimentary, and delighted that we were allies fighting our common enemy. They were aware of the direction of my work and said they had a friend in Russia going along the same road.

Clem told me their friend would love to compare notes with me, or, failing that, to be allowed a glimpse or preview of work of mine that had not yet been published. Vlad popped in the information that their friend was very very rich and always expressed his gratitude with generosity.

Was I well paid, they asked in their direct disarming Russian style.

'Of course not,' I replied. 'England never rewards its intelligentsia. Every Englishman thinks that no one is cleverer than he is. Brains earn not much more than brawn, possibly less on average.'

They laughed, they thought I was joking, and carried the joke further.

'But you don't need money – money is the dirty word – you work for love and glory,' Clem said, and Vlad chimed in: 'Let the peasants eat the cake! Our diet will be fresh air on toast with margarine.'

When they had stopped laughing, Clem inquired: 'Please, I would like to know, what is a lot of money?'

I hesitated.

He proceeded: 'Is two thousand pounds a little, money?'

'That's big money.'

Vlad glanced at Clem, then said with his melancholy smile: 'Our friend shows appreciation with big thanks.'

Clem had the creamy voice of a fat man and an easy attractive manner. He looked straight at me, straighter than usual, and came to the point.

'We wish to ask a favour,' he said. 'Our friend would be grateful if you would share your research with him, as intelligence was shared universally before patents and wars came between good people.'

Vlad dealt with practicalities.

'If you would meet us with papers, I would take photographs in our car while you went walking with Clem. Then you would get your papers back with our friend's present. We know that your research is not of strategic value. We would give you guarantees that if your work was useful to our friend, you would receive credit for it, for example in book or professional magazine.'

Clem put the finishing touch to this rigmarole.

'You must think carefully. But please, because we go away soon, meet us tomorrow to tell your decisions.'

We parted. My thoughts revolved exclusively around Carol. Some hours passed and I again knocked on her door. I invited her to walk down to the pub. She began to search for an excuse, but I stopped her, insisted so far as I was able, emphasised the importance of the outing, and obtained agreement.

We stayed in the pub for no more than half an hour, then retraced the steps we had taken on a different night, a night illuminated by the moon and by kisses. We did not touch, nor had we touched since she taught me to kiss; and neither of us had referred to her pregnancy.

Now, in the dark, as planned, I said to her: 'I know you're having a baby.'

After a strained silence she murmured: 'Bill told you.'

'What are you going to do, Carol?'

I heard her sniff.

'Carol, I love you, I'd marry you if you'd say the word, I'd look after you and give the baby my name.'

'You can't – how can you? – I'd ruin you.'
'I can and I will.'
'But your career...'
'I've spoken, Carol.'
'But I've been so nasty to you.'
'Well – I've spoken.'
'Oh – Alan!'

Mistake Compounded

Carol was older than me, and shrewder – she was a woman after all; even so late in the day I cannot quite bring myself to pay her a compliment.

She was responsible for my fall. But truth and accuracy would deny it. I proposed to marry her. I wanted to be her husband not only for charitable reasons. I allowed heart or other bodily organs to govern head for a change.

Initially, nocturnally, she inspired my hopes of love. She amused herself by kissing a virginal man with an obsessive nature. She then succumbed to Bill Hendrix, was careless, chose to become a little girl lost, whom I was typecast by one adulterer or perhaps by both to find and rescue. To suit themselves, whether or not in unison, they steered me to the top of the cliff, and Bill sent along Clem and Vlad to push me over the edge.

But, again, I was at liberty not to keep the second assignation with the Russians. I could have said in the café, where it was suggested, that I was not meeting anyone in a wood in the middle of nowhere to hand over my lifework to date, thus breaking the law governing secret information and my vow of confidentiality.

Yes, in the café, surely I was still free.

Yet doubtless truth would cavil by referring to Bill's assurances that I was not to worry about money, money was no problem, and to the subsequent bribe that was placed before me, virtually upon the stained oilcloth covering that café table. Greed for money, for power over Carol, enslaved me without difficulty or delay: they promised that she was as good as mine, she would have to stop saying no – her alternative to yes was to embrace the prevailing predicament of single parenthood.

My personal relations with my fiancée are easy to record. They were nil. I gave her an engagement ring – we gave each other nothing else. There were pecks but not kisses, pecks that hurt. She was torn between gratitude and resentment to be so beholden to me. How she justified her agreement to be my wife, I never knew. She sometimes thanked but did not repay me for sparing her rejection by her parents, general embarrassment, the loss of her present job, poverty, homelessness. Each day, each night of our engagement raised only fading hopes.

Colleagues did not help. Most guessed that funny business was afoot and moderated their congratulations. The older man whom we called Grandad took me aside to ask if Carol understood the importance of my work; and another old boy spoke to Carol, telling her to provide space and silence in which to enable me to fulfil my potential. Arthur, my friend, was disturbingly candid.

'She'll stop you working.'

'She won't.'

'You're too young to marry.'

'Why do you say that? How do you know?'

'Can you afford to be a husband and father?'

'That's my business, Arthur.'

'What do your parents think?'

Arthur was typical: he conformed to a type of genius in that he understood one big thing, physics, and almost nothing else. Although unburdened by common knowledge, he was still able to put his finger on the weak links of my situation.

I broke the news to my mother.

'Oh no,' she moaned. 'Have you thought of all the trouble you'll have when there are children to look after and feed? Oh Alan, what will become of your career? Now you'll be having no sleep at night and money worries.'

Father was equally gloomy.

'We didn't expect you to be running after skirt,' he said. 'Your mother and I waited to marry till we were older and wiser. Carol's a dietician, you say. Any rate, that must mean she'll give you the right things to eat.'

Carol in person failed to dispel my parents' reservations. I was aware that she was inhibited by the fibs she had to tell; but they thought she was snooty and ungracious.

'She doesn't seem to be happy, Alan,' Mother said to me; and Father opined that she looked wilful.

Carol, too, had criticisms to air and displease me.

'They think I'll kill you,' she said.

'No, they don't,' I lied. 'Please don't worry.'

'They're probably right.'

'No, they're not.'

'You can still back out, Alan – I'll cope.'

'I'm not going to.'

My meeting with her parents was another bad day.

They were snobs. They suspected me of presumption. Her mother was worse than my bank manager. Where was the money coming from, she demanded. I was to understand that the effect of the war on her family's circumstances boiled down to no dowry for Carol – nothing doing in the monetary line, she warned me. Her father expressed the hope that our marriage was not a shotgun affair – or was he threatening?

We agreed to a white wedding, notwithstanding war, clothes rationing, shortages of petrol, and, more importantly, Carol's lack of religion and my rejection of God and His representative in Rome. We did so to counteract the impression that it was hasty, forced, convenient, one-sided. We made our promises in a little local church in front of a score or so of people, and afterwards had drinks at the pub near Camp X.

We spent our honeymoon in the tiny cottage I had bought with part of the Russians' money. Strange to relate, I had worried about every single aspect of my marriage excepting the wherewithal that made the match. As the previous pages have implied and illustrate, my conscience is serviceable, to put it politely. I thank my parents for my intelligence and robust constitution and nervous system. But I inherited something from my father that I never asked for and am not proud of. He was an upright man, a pillar of his church, a moral authority within the castle of our home. But he obtained coal from the mill that employed him and overlooked the fact that he was stealing it.

Our cottage was within easy bicycling distance of Camp X, and we both had bicycles. Carol tried to work office hours; but punctual time-keeping was not enforced, and, when she was afraid her swelling figure was noticeable and would prompt observers to count telltale days and months, she often left early to do shopping and prepare dinner for the two of us, although we could get meals in the canteen. One evening, I returned home at about eight-thirty and she opened our front door as if to welcome me; but then I saw mixed expressions on her face. She seemed to be waiting to tell me news that was bad.

What had happened?

'Guess what we're having for supper!'

61

I tried and eventually gave up.

'Okay – tell me!'

'Caviare.'

The shock was terrible. I had been shocked before. I was much more shocked by the caviare – my blood pressure must have doubled, I felt a rush of blood to the face, sweated, and was amazed that Carol did not notice.

It was two shocks in one. First, it was a sort of delayed penalty. Incredibly maybe, but truthfully, my dealings with Clem and Vlad had not worried me unduly. We had played a game, which I had won to the tune of two thousand pounds. The exchange was fair, was mutual assistance – that was the beginning and end of the matter, I had assumed, expected, hoped or taken for granted. Since then Carol had preoccupied me, Carol and the struggle to please her.

In a flash I saw my mistake and the consequences stretching ahead.

At the same time, I inferred, dared to guess, that Bill Hendrix must be a spy. It had occurred to me that he was solving the problem of my finance, never that he himself was engaged in the trade of secrets. My second shock was finding that I had stumbled into a hall of mirrors, a new nightmare world of deception.

I asked a silly question.

'How did you come by caviare?'

'Two men called here. They brought presents, wedding presents, caviare and Russian cigarettes. They said they were friends of yours.'

'They're not my friends, they belonged to the Hendrix circus. But I got to know them slightly. They're called Clam and Vlad. Vlad's short for Vladimir, Clem's name defeats me.'

'I thought they were sinister.'

'Well, they're Russians.'

'Have you ever tasted caviare?'

'Yes – we ate it constantly at Thornwick. Have you ever eaten it?'

'No. I don't think I'd like it. It smells fishy. They smelt fishy to me.'

'They're only a couple of dons from Portugal doing research at University Y, they're harmless.'

'They would have stayed on here to see you, but I'd had enough of their hand-kissing and compliments after half an hour and shooed them out.'

'I'm glad you did.'

'They said they'd be back anyway.'

'What?'

'They said they'd be back.'

'Did they?'

That Carol did not understand my final query was a cry of alarm was an unintentional comment on the state of our marriage.

Later, we tasted the caviare, which stuck in my throat – she loved it. We also smoked the peculiar cigarettes with elongated hollow mouthpieces. Tobacco was supposed to be good for nerves in those days, and during the war most people smoked every smokeable substance they could get hold of. Russian cigarettes did not soothe my nerves.

The game I had played with Clem and Vlad was punishable by death, as had been proved in certain high profile cases since the war began. I had not been only a fool: I was a criminal. My mistake was irreparable. I had sold my freedom twice over, and for ever, first by selling my work, then by using the money to marry. I had sold my birthright for the mess of potage of vowing to be Carol's husband until death parted us.

She was not a bad girl, I suppose, let alone a wicked woman. Her pregnancy was an illness and never gave us much of a chance. She would have been lovely if she had loved me and been well, and had not got caught out by obliging her partner in adultery. She was tougher than she would have been if she had not felt so guilty and sad to be married to me and not to Bill.

There was only one bedroom in our home, with space for only one bed scarcely wide enough for two. She would neither let me touch her nor would she touch me.

'Don't – please – can't you control yourself?... I told you, you were warned – go away, get lost' – such was our night life.

I fell out of that bed, or slept on the floor, or downstairs on two chairs, or worked instead of sleeping.

We never discussed the why and wherefore of our life together. We hardly discussed anything: we were both dog-tired for rather different reasons. Yet, although Carol cried a lot, she could and would reveal an authoritarian streak, and boss and scold me.

She obeyed stricter rules than I recognised. She was my social superior, if only by a slender margin, and she carried cleanliness and daintiness to what I regarded as extremes. She insisted on my use of a nail-brush. She would decant marmalade from a jar into a glass dish. She was critical of absent-minded professors who did not have their hair cut and wore their pyjamas under their suits.

She was more political than me. She disapproved of the trades unionists in vital industries – in mining, in the docks – who struck for higher wages while our soldiers fought and died on battlefields. She was patriotic and belligerent, and believed scare stories of German parachutists roaming our countryside in nuns' habits. She was suspicious of the USSR, which had signed treaties with Hitler even if it was now fighting against him and for us. That she had morals, and was probably more moral for the sake of her unborn child, put additional strain on her relationship with the man she never loved.

All this, the loveless cohabitation, the emerging features of her character, combined with the dread of her discovery of what I had done, and dread of what was in store and what I might have to do, forced me to think the unthinkable: I wanted out, as they say in Scotland.

It was impossible – everything was impossible.

We got through the remaining months of her pregnancy. The delivery of the child would take place in the hospital of the town some twelve miles from our cottage. The ambulance service was alerted, and we had a fallback plan involving a district nurse with a car. Carol was nonetheless, and naturally, apprehensive. She allowed me to go to work, but begged me to return punctually. For a week or so I had left Camp X at about four-thirty and bicycled the four miles home as fast I could.

When the birth was already three days overdue, I left Camp X at four twenty-five on the afternoon in question. I was cycling along the lane through the wood where I had met Clem and Vlad for the last time, and spotted their car. It was parked on the verge, a black Ford station wagon. They saw me coming and stepped out, smiling and waving, while my heart sank.

'Hullo, good day, good afternoon,' they said, together with words of welcome in Russian.

I had to stop, but said I was rushing home in case my wife had started having her baby.

Vlad returned, as if he had not heard me: 'Our friend wishes me to thank you very very much for your kind assistance. He sent you presents – you received his presents? They were to thank you and your charming wife.'

'Yes, yes – thank you, thank him – but my wife...'

'Please!' Clem weighed in. 'One minute will not make difference. Our friend would like more help.'

'I'm sorry, I can't – no more, nothing more.'

Vlad said: 'We will talk again.'

'No,' I repeated. 'I'm not giving you any more papers, nothing.'

Vlad contradicted me in his deep growl: 'Giving, no – selling, yes, buying, yes.' And he laughed as he asked the usual question that foreigners tack on to their questions: 'No?'

I said I must go.

Clem said: 'We will see you soon.'

'No, don't – our business is finished, finished!'

'Hurry to your wife,' Vlad said, 'and please give her our best greetings and wishes.'

I pedalled away. But I was angry and scared, my heart began to thump and miss beats, and as soon as I was out of sight of the Russians I stopped and sat down on the verge with my head between my knees. I could not have done otherwise – had been afraid I would die – and have no accurate recollection of the passage of time.

Carol was in our garden, lying half in and half out of a flowerbed. She was in great pain and had not been able to reach the telephone.

'How long, how long?' I kept on asking as I supported her indoors, meaning how long had she been lying there in the open.

Her answer cut deep.

'You were late,' she said.

Carol's baby was born and baptised in the church where we married in spite of all the obstacles in the way of such an event.

It was a boy, and she gave him the first names Alexander William. I probed into neither, but guessed that the Alexander referred to the victory against the odds that he had won.

Carol had no time for, or interest in, anyone or anything but Alexander. Two or three weeks elapsed before I had an opportunity to apologise for missing my cue to help her with the performance of his birth.

'It doesn't matter,' she said, but then asked: 'What kept you?'

'My work,' I replied.

'Oh yes, your work.'

Her dismissiveness grated. She should not have sneered at my occupation – setting aside my sensibilities, she probably owed her son to it and certainly her security. She seemed to have forgotten that her collapse in the garden and the pains of parturition were her own affair. My late arrival was almost my right, not my wrong that she predictably tried to make out that it was.

Then I remembered Clem and Vlad. I had let myself be detained by men who had paid to gain a hold over me. There was more wrong with my arrival on the scene of Carol's labour than I had believed and than she knew.

The loneliness of the husband of a mother with her first child increased the loneliness of a husband unloved by his wife and unloving, and I had to get away from Carol. I might be able to justify my conduct to myself somehow or other, even if it was sure to be unjustifiable in her shrewd eyes. Without her, I might be able to do my work and follow my star, and find the strength to repulse the Russians.

I reckoned without the professionals, whose knowledge of pressure points was positively oriental.

Those sleepless nights of which my mother had warned me were exhausting. My work had suffered, and indecision and pessimism were taking another toll of my energy. And Clem and Vlad ambushed me again.

Their Ford was parked on the side of the road near the bottom of the drive to Camp

X. They were standing beside it in such a way that I could not swerve on my bicycle and pass by. I was furious, afraid I would be seen in their company, had to dismount, and demanded as forcefully as I dared: 'What are you doing here?'

They congratulated me on becoming the father of a son: how did they know so much – or so little?

'You shouldn't be here,' I told them.

'But we are on a public road, Alan,' Clem explained.

Vlad had a more sympathetic explanation to offer his accomplice: 'No – Alan is anxious, he would prefer to meet us privately.' He turned to me and said: 'But we are only cementing the alliance of our two countries – you have no cause to worry.'

'We could talk in the car,' Clem suggested to Vlad, and Vlad agreed by saying: 'We have room for the bicycle.'

It was like a kidnap: my bike was taken from me and stowed in the back of the station wagon, I was led by the hand into the front passenger seat, Clem climbed in behind me and Vlad drove off.

The speed of these developments confused me.

Clem was leaning forward and speaking

into my ear.

'We wish to reassure you, Alan. You are a brilliant man, and an honourable man. We respect you greatly, so does our friend in Moscow. None of us would involve you in dishonourable business, or wish you to suspect that we are exposing you to trouble or risk.'

Vlad said: 'You are English, we are Russian, and now we are friends. Russia admires England, its great history, arts, courage and even some of its politics, but we are a new country, an old country with new politics, we are for the future. And you have helped us, Alan, and we are very very grateful to you.'

Clem took up the cudgels.

'Our friend would be even more grateful if you would help again. He would like to see the conclusion of your work that he has already seen. But it is his request, our request, no more. You will do as you please, Alan.'

'That is correct, Alan,' Vlad growled; 'We ask but you will answer.'

'My answer's no – and I would like you to stop the car and give me back my bicycle.'

They did not argue. They obeyed and indulged me. They pretended to be putty in my hands. The car stopped. I repeated that

I was selling no more of my work, not another fraction. They smiled at me and shook my hand warmly. I bicycled home as fast as I could.

This episode is not so frightening in the form of a written recollection as it was in reality. Every soft word uttered in that car sounded to me like its opposite, and seemed to bind and gag me preparatory to torture or harsh punishment.

Some time passed, days probably. The USA was now fighting our war as well as their own with Japan. Hitler had succeeded not only in conquering a large part of the world, but also in uniting and antagonising the strangest of gigantic bedfellows, communism and capitalism.

The subject debated at Camp X was whether the UK would or should be saved from the Nazi menace by the USSR or the USA. My nature was apolitical, I had never had time for politics, and now had reason to keep quiet; but a version of the controversy crept into our cottage.

Carol was unimpressed by the USSR, to put it mildly. Women in general and pretty ones in particular are seldom impressed by egalitarian experiments – they are born competitors and would-be elitists. On the other hand she associated the USA with films, tough guys, big open spaces and a comprehensible language.

On occasions, as we listened to news broadcasts, I would speak up for the political side that I had favoured and been favoured by.

For instance I voiced admiration for the defenders of Stalingrad. Carol said: 'I hope the Nazis kill the Bolshies and vice versa – I hope it'll be good riddance to bad rubbish.'

'Don't you want our ally to win?' I asked.

'Some ally! When they've polished off the Germans they'll kill all of us.'

'That's silly – the Russians aren't keen on exporting their revolution any more.'

'So they may say. But the commies at Camp X were always squirming about, searching wastepaper baskets and trying to get hold of information by hook or by crook. I wouldn't put anything past them.'

'Oh Carol, that's just Reds-under-the-beds politics!'

'But they *are* under the beds, and in the beds, they're everywhere. You're so naive, you're such an innocent! I hate England for its muddle-through attitude! Why does it have to be so arrogant and pitiful at the same time? You'll wake up when it's too late,

Alan, and discover how untrustworthy the Russians are.'

Sometimes our arguments grew heated. The sad truth was that they generated more passion than the rest of our relationship. Carol would still not sleep with me or offer me any physical sign of affection. She was an extreme case of the syndrome of gratitude breeding hatred; and was allowed no room for manoeuvre by that unyielding chin of hers. The cottage with its garden and picket fence was not the setting for a rural idyll, far from it: for me it was strictly a lodging, and for my wife and her child a fortified refuge.

The illness of Alexander William served a purpose similar to our divergent politics, it broke the ice between us. I was consulted and expected to supply comfort. But the illness suddenly threatened the child's life, and, when the crisis subsided, left him with an unusual physical defect. Carol agonised and pleaded with all and sundry for assistance. A surgeon in London specialised in the operation that was required; but there was no National Health Service in those days, and his fee was beyond our means. Parents and friends offered contributions; but, again, their pennies and ours did not add up to the total expense, and Carol hated to beg, especially when money was so tight thanks to the war. One awful evening in our cottage she cried for hours on end, not boohooing, just facing me with tears rolling down her cheeks while she wrung her hands as if washing them, and not responding to any of my strictly verbal efforts to alleviate her misery.

After she had gone upstairs to bed, taking her baby with her, I reviewed my circumstances and my options.

Later, because I could not bear things as they were, and saw a last chance of changing them for the better, because of pity and politics, I rang the telephone number Clem and Vlad had forced upon me.

I received the money in cash, as before. It was half the previous payment, one thousand pounds, but enough. I put it in another envelope, sealed the envelope, wrote on it, 'With my love', and gave it to Carol on the evening after the awful one.

She was disbelieving. Equally, her thankfulness was almost incredible. She melted. She embraced me, soaked me with her tears of unqualified gratitude, guilt on account of her nastiness to me, bewilderment over her inability to reciprocate my feelings or to reward me for my kindness, and wretchedness now tinged with hope.

Before bedtime she kissed me as she had once before. It was like a payment on account. She promised me that when Alexander William was well again, when the trauma of her recent history had healed, and I was perhaps ready and willing to begin all over again, she would do her best to make up for the past. We were still so young, she said, we had a long time ahead in which to make love.

The next day at work she rang me to say she had fixed an emergency appointment with the Harley Street specialist and was going to London. She had friends there, she would stay with them for as long as Alexander's treatment lasted. Was that okay, would I manage, she added superfluously.

They returned ten days later. I had received only one communication, a postcard telling me the operation had been successful and giving me their approximate time of arrival. I waited for them, having bought food and flowers. I was more excited than I can describe.

She was colder to me than ever. She was angry with me – I could see it, I knew it, although no explanation was forthcoming immediately. She did not acknowledge the flowers. She took Alexander upstairs to bed as soon as she had fed him.

Then she joined and attacked me.

Where had that money come from?

'Don't ask,' I replied. 'I gave it to you on condition no questions were asked.'

'I knew nothing about conditions. You set no conditions. I want an answer to my question.'

'I'm setting the conditions now.'

'No go, Alan! Those notes were used. The surgeon asked me if I'd robbed a bank. I was embarrassed – you hadn't even warned me. What were you doing with a thousand used pound notes?'

'I'm not answering, Carol.'

'Did you steal them?'

'Of course!'

'It's no joke!'

'I'm not joking, and I'm not telling you.'

'Are you doing something too bad to tell me?'

'That depends. Anyway, you took the money, you spent it. You're my accomplice whatever I did or didn't do. If you suspected me of such a bad crime, why didn't you give me back the money you think I got hold of criminally?'

That point changed the direction of our quarrel. She prided herself on her probity.

'What have you let us in for?' she wailed.

But again tempers flared.

She said: 'I won't stand by you, Alan, if you've committed a crime. Don't think I'll lie for you. And I'm not linking my life with someone who's keeping secrets from me.'

'It's no good your taking that high and mighty line. Leave it alone, Carol! Let sleeping dogs, and so on. I will make one admission, and I advise you to pay attention. You're no holier than I am.'

'Is that all?'

'Yes.'

'Oh God! I know I've not been nice to you, but I really wanted to stop being nasty. And now you're informing me that I'm in potential trouble without telling me what or why or when. Was I as cruel to you as you're being to me?'

'Shut up – do as you're told – I'm sick of your nonsense – go and be with Bill Hendrix's spawn!'

'Oh no! No!'

'Leave me be, Carol!'

She cried. But they were tears of rage. She was soon hacking away at me with every available weapon.

Bill had never been so foul as I was being. Bill was a gentleman whereas I was a feeble highbrow who had never had a woman. She attributed some of her frigidity to the fear that I would prove to be impotent. She had never dreamt of being married to a conjurer who could pull used pound notes out of the air. She accused me of theft, fraud, armed robbery, and then of selfishness.

That she could think me selfish was unacceptable.

I demanded evidence.

'You're not selfish in the ordinary sense,' she granted, 'but it's selfish of you to send me off to London with money that looks like loot and refuse to explain.'

'Very well,' said I, casting caution aside; 'if you want an explanation, get it from Bill.'

'From Bill?'

'You heard me.'

'What's Bill to do with it? Of course, he gave you the money.'

'Think what you like.'

'Are you saying he didn't give you the money? He refused to give it even for his own son?'

I shrugged.

'Did you go to Bill? Tell me that at least!'

'No.'

'Are you saying you didn't go?'

'No – I'm refusing to tell you anything more.'

'Are you and Bill doing something dishonest together?'

'Shut up, Carol!'

'Are you selling classified information?'

'Oh for pity's sake!'

'Bill was always too rich. Was it all jiggery-pokery?'

'I can't answer for Bill, and I'm not answering for myself.'

'I hate you!'

'That's as may be, Carol. But I've saved your bacon twice over, and you don't pay your debts.'

'How can I? If you've done what I think you've done, we could both be shot. It's no good, Alan – sorry! All I know is that our marriage is well and truly over.'

'Yes.'

'You do see that, don't you?'

'Yes.'

'I'm sorry.'

'So am I.'

'Good night, Alan.'

I spent the rest of that night weighing the pros and cons of suicide. But in the morning I went to work before she had shown a sign of life. Camp X had given her leave of absence so that she could care for Alexander: in the course of the day after our final quarrel she tendered her resignation by telephone and moved out of our cottage and in with a female Camp X friend.

I heard news of her. She found a job that suited, she worked in the canteen of a camp for American soldiers in the vicinity – there were amenities for her child and she was unlikely to bump into me. Apparently, she did not contact Bill. Later on she lived with a Texan captain, and, after our divorce came through, she married him and ended up in Texas.

The Set-up

My break with Carol had repercussions. I was not permitted to nurse my wounds in solitude and silence.

Our cottage – now mine – was located in a narrow lane. Not many cars passed by, the drivers were not keen to meet other vehicles head on. There were fields in front and a village visible across more fields from the back. I had no close neighbours, and the isolation suited me – I already had a reason to be reclusive when I bought the place.

But I was never sociable. My work was my life, although I had hoped that Carol would be my companion and partner as well as my wife. Without her, I wanted no one, and resigned myself to chance meetings with colleagues at Camp X.

One evening the Ford station wagon was parked by my garden gate. I had bicycled home, and it was waiting for me.

I shouted at the two men in the front seats: 'You can't stay there, go away, go!'

Clem and Vlad got out of the car, smiling and with hands outstretched.

'Go away,' I shouted.

Clem replied in his plump oily voice: 'We are so sorry that your wife is no longer with you.'

'We are sorry, too, that she has taken away your son,' Vlad growled.

'How do you know where my wife is? You don't understand anything. Go away, please! Nothing doing, no more papers ever, I've told you and I'm repeating it because you're so pig-headed.'

'What is pig-headed?' Vlad asked Clem,

and Clem told Vlad, 'We must do as our sad friend wishes.'

'I am not sad – what I am is not your business – goodbye, *adieu* – and that's final!'

They shook my hand. They looked like the sad ones – their looks were always deceptive. Deliberately they got back into the car, and drove away at a snail's pace, as if from a scene of tragedy.

My truer friend Arthur brought his logic to bear upon my situation.

'Marriage and paternity are distractions,' he ruled. 'Your output will show a profit because of what you consider your loss.'

'Thanks for the sympathy, Arthur.'

'Carol's a dietician. I fail to see what good she could ever be to you, apart from supervising your diet.'

'Do you make no allowances for love? Do you recognise the emotion called love?'

'I do not. I recognise lust and copulation. Euphemisms are of no interest to science. Love's an indisposition, usually temporary although it can become chronic. The symptoms are a form of vertigo, vertigo of the intelligence, which can do lasting damage, personal and widespread.'

'Well, you're a doctor, albeit the wrong sort of doctor, so what's the cure for it in your opinion?'

'Work it out of your system, avoid it in future, come back to live at Camp X, and rededicate yourself to the pursuit of knowledge and excellence.'

My parents' comfort was even colder than Arthur's, and my sister took advantage of her opportunity to kick me.

Mother tested my self-control by harping on the fate of my son and her grandson. When I asked her not to, she worried Carol in the canine sense – shook her, tore her to ribbons, skinned her alive so far as was possible. Then she turned on me.

'You've been a fool to yourself, Alan. And you've deprived me of a grandson. But it's your business, I suppose. How much has it cost you? Where did you find the money? It's wasted now, that's a fact. You must have spent every penny of your savings. What a disappointment for all of us!'

Father was even more financial.

'We were counting on you to repay us with interest for all the help we gave you,' he explained. 'You're still young. You'll make money one day, I shouldn't wonder. I won't be working much longer, son, and I'll thank you to think of how you'll give us a helping hand in our turn.'

Ethel said to me in private: 'So your fancy woman's thought better of you! I don't blame her – she must have found a man more manly than you are – it wouldn't be difficult. Stick to your books and dirty magazines, that's my advice!'

At least Carol's parents kept quiet.

And at least Carol did not return to probe and pester me.

I crouched in the cottage, punishing myself with my solitude, while recognising that I was getting off lightly in a worldly sense. Often, diffidently, I remembered my religion; but I felt unworthy to communicate with God, and, at the same time, rejected Roman Catholicism all over again because I could not trust the priests I would have to confess to, and therefore could not obtain absolution.

The war was grinding to its close. Some people, at Camp X and elsewhere, said that America had won it for us. I contended, was forced to contend, that the USSR was saving the civilisation of the Western World – I had taken its shilling, committed myself to it, and closed my ears to stories of its rapine and pillage.

For time best forgotten my existence seemed to hang from a naked electric wire as yet unelectrified. I worked, slept, sought to lose myself in whatever had to be done, and dreamed, while living in constant fear of the electric shock that would hurt, wound, maim, kill me.

There was no escape. The wire running through every hour of every day and much of my nights was my association with Clem and Vlad. Carol was not malicious – she had asked for none of my money in her petition for divorce, and I trusted her not to blab her suspicions from the housetops or betray me – and possibly the father of her child. But a word, a hint, dropped by the Russians could be my undoing – a word to a friend who had friends who had connections with authority or the law; and I had no power to shut their mouths for ever or control them in any way.

My emotions revolved round Clem and Vlad. They had set me sphinx-like riddles. Were they full-blown spies rather than dons? What was their connection with Bill Hendrix? What part had Bill really played in the second chapter of my story? Could he be the exact opposite of the person he appeared to be? And who was the friend, the Muscovite, we were all apparently working for? I could supply no answers. The overriding fact was that they, my Reds, had absolute power over me, and I wished them at the bottom of the sea.

On another evening, an evening in summer, about eight o'clock, my doorbell rang. I jumped to conclusions and hid in the kitchen. My heart thumped – I hear it still – I was so frightened and furious. The doorbell rang again. I did not move from where I stood, out of sight of ground floor windows, front and back. Silence fell.

But the kitchen window was open and a voice called through it, 'Anyone at home?' – a girl's voice, lilting and cheerful.

I answered. I met a young woman – about my age, fine fuller figure, brown hair sprouting and flopping over her forehead, bright eyes, rosy cheeks, bearing a resemblance to a Scottish terrier. She told me her name, Erica – very modern, no mention of surname. We were speaking through the kitchen window. She explained herself.

'I hope you don't mind my calling. Someone I studied with told me where you lived. He said you might not mind my saying hullo. I've been abroad, and only just returned to England – I'm bicycling round to get my bearings again.'

You could not help liking her, I certainly

could not, she was so friendly. I suppose I more than liked her at first sight, because she flustered me, she affected me as the footprint in the sand affected Robinson Crusoe, and despite my interrogative nature I omitted to ask any questions.

I invited her in. We went to lock her bicycle to the fence and collect her saddle-bag for safety's sake. I said I could offer her eggs and a rasher of bacon for supper – it was supper-time. She accepted with enthusiasm – she would cook the eggs for me and repay my kindness. She was thirsty and I gave her gin and lemonade, and she used my lavatory, and hunted for utensils in my kitchen, and cooked a delicious meal in a delicious manner, and talked, joked, laughed, drank her half of a precious bottle of wine, and blew all the cobwebs away.

She was heading for a youth hostel where she would sleep. She did not mind if the hostel had no bed for her – she had a sleeping bag and would doss down in a field under the stars or in a barn. Discomfort meant nothing to her – she believed she could never be unhappy again now that the war was over.

She was very flattering. I felt like a tin god when she spoke of the privilege of not only meeting the author of my books but also eating with him. It was heady stuff after Carol's inhibitions and the criticism I had been exposed to. Erica had made a long detour to find my cottage. She loved the simplicity of my home, was pleasantly surprised that I did not live in a palace, and expatiated on the charms of my kitchen with its antiquated range and my sitting-room with sticks and twigs stacked by the fire for use in the winter.

'It's cosy here... You're such a good host... I am not disappointed, quite the opposite... How can I thank you?'

Dusk fell, and we sat on at the kitchen table. We spoke in general terms of the war, the waste, the heroism, the awfulness of the Nazis and the tyrannies of the Right, Franco as well as Hitler.

'The Russians are my heroes,' she said, and we drank a toast to them together.

'Oh my goodness, look how dark it is,' she exclaimed. 'I must leave you at once, I've got miles to bicycle.'

We stood up. But she stumbled and lost her balance.

'I've drunk too much,' she said. 'How terrible – so sorry!'

'You can't bicycle anywhere tonight,' I said.

'Would you let me sleep in your garden? Oh dear!'

She stumbled again and I had to catch her. She giggled, we were both laughing, but she pressed against me and we stopped laughing and gazed at each other. Her face with shadowy eye sockets and the glint of a white tooth showing between her parted lips was infinitely romantic and seductive. We kissed once, twice, times without number. She led me upstairs, she had been upstairs earlier. She carried her saddlebag in her free hand, and in the bathroom availed herself of the necessities. In the bed I had never shared with Carol, under the covers, and over the covers, this way and that, I was initiated into the rites of love, which we made intermittently until long after dawn.

We left the cottage together in the morning. We pedalled away on our bicycles, Erica to meet friends by arrangement, I to clock in late at Camp X – not exactly poetic, but only after further demonstrations of affection, declarations, regrets and promises.

For a day or two, for several days so bewitched by tentative joy and hope that I cannot remember how many, I tried to adjust to the condition of being alone but lonely no longer. Better late, wonderfully although late, I had found love or it had found me. And it proved that I was not a masochist, thrilled by the pain of entrusting my heart to Carol, nor a bodiless brain like Arthur, whose desires were satisfied by algebraic formulae, nor a kind of dustman, fated to clear up the messes made by better men.

At last my cap had its sexual feather. Erica was higher on the scale of lovability than Carol: physically she brimmed over, she was stronger, in smoother working order, more outgoing, and jollier. I was prouder of Erica than I would have been of Carol even if the latter had been my mate instead of my wife. Moreover I sensed that Erica was cleverer, which was at least a relief, although it was not her top storey that was her main attraction.

I had told her more about myself than she had told me. She was an orphan; she had lost her parents somewhere in North Africa – her father had worked in that part of the world; she had no other relations anywhere, but had been brought up by a godfather or god-mother in one of the African states not involved in the war. She was a student of languages – she spoke Russian fluently and had done some simultaneous Russian-English translation; she was one of nature's gypsies, she lived to roam, for new experiences, for change and excitement. I knew no more at that stage – the rest of our verbal communications had been pillow talk.

The extraordinary thing was her implication or claim that her foot-loose tendencies had been her own version of the search for a great love – in other words, which I blush to write, for me. Her compliments did not stop downstairs – her praises of my performance could be called beginner's luck. It was nonetheless music to my ears, and stimulating at the same time.

The happiness of my recollections waned as anxiety as to whether or not I would ever see her again waxed. Without her, and the future she dangled before my imagination, I would not be persuaded that life was worth living. But she kept her word. She blew in and again the cobwebs were put to flight.

She stayed with me for as long as she could, a weekend perhaps – she had other plans and commitments, and, as I could not leave my work for good reasons, she missed me and was out of a job during the days. Half of our reunion was spent in commiserating over the goodbyes in store. We agreed wryly that absence did increase the fondness of our hearts. I proposed marriage, but she said she was too young and it would bring our magic roundabout to a halt. We were happy beyond description and then knew the sweetness of the sorrows of separating.

We never disagreed. Our tastes dovetailed in the mental and moral as well as the physical context. She was boldly Marxist, though not a card-carrying member of the Communist Party, and again I followed where she led, after she had laughed at me for being a Laodician, neither hot nor cold politically. It was not a big step for me, not that I told or even dreamed of telling her why. We spoke with excitement of the possibilities opened up by the war – the conquest of the world by the will of the people, and the end of the cruel competitiveness of capitalism. But politics did not interrupt our embraces, nor did the forthcoming battles in the streets sully the peace we achieved in our little heaven on earth.

Our love cast no shadow until we were standing in the roadway, Erica by her bicycle and myself seeing her off. It was a sunny morning, and we had promised each other to be brave, not sad. I detained her with extra kisses, then asked an unnecessary question.

She had explained that she was meeting

people in the UK in order to gather copy for the required thesis for her doctorate. My question was unnecessary because it was completely beside the point of our *au revoirs*. I asked which university she studied at – I knew it was abroad, but where?

'Portugal,' she replied.

She stayed away longer. More to the point, she returned. Everything would have been the same, but for the doubts boiling up and almost over in my mind.

At the kitchen table on the first evening of that third visit, after we had eaten and were otherwise satisfied and fulfilled, I asked another question: 'The friend who suggested you should call on me – do you remember?'

'I'll never forget,' she said.

'Who was it?'

'It,' she laughed, 'was my tutor and teacher' – and she reeled off a Russian surname with a professional prefix.

'Is it a man?'

We laughed together.

'Yes, it is. He's here, at University Y, and he's met you once or twice. He's very nice, he's a Russian who is good.'

'What's his first name?'

'Clemens.'

'Oh. Oh yes – Clem to me – we have met. Do you know his chum?'

'Vladimir, you mean?'

'I call him Vlad – I never knew their full names – they were Clem and Vlad to me.'

'Vladimir is another good Russian who thinks as we do. Did you ever talk politics with those two?'

'Not really.'

'They're interesting. They're not just *apparatchiks* – they've got minds of their own. How did you know them, Alan?'

'Through people called Hendrix – Bill Hendrix used to work at Camp X.'

'Oh yes.'

'Do you know Bill, Erica?'

'No. I may have heard his name. I was wondering – would you like to ask your Clem and Vlad to dinner one evening?'

'No – it wouldn't be a good idea.'

'Why not? It would be fun.'

'It's security – at Camp X we have to be careful – fraternising with Russians could be frowned on.'

'That's ridiculous! Churchill has fraternised with Stalin. What's wrong with you entertaining a Russian professor of Linguistics who's lived and worked in Portugal for years?'

'There's nothing wrong, but I don't want to get involved with the security people.'

'You could say boo to them.'

'Honestly, I've better things to do than pick a fight.'

'Oh, very well. But I still think it's silly.'

'Listen, if you would like to see Clem, that'd be different. Of course he could come here. You asked me if I would like it, and I was giving my view.'

'Thank you, Alan. You're very sweet. But it doesn't matter to me – I'd like best to do whatever you like. So bye-bye, Clemens and Vladimir! We'll be happier by ourselves.'

She was nearly right. Her character was big and generous, and she did not sulk. She overlooked or refused to see the shadow I had seen. It was not her fault that she was not in on my secret, which made the exchange about a minor social engagement more stressful for me than for her.

I tried to follow her example. And I must add that her example was hard not to follow. She preoccupied, she monopolised me. She was no longer my guest, she was never like a guest, she was my mentor, my leader. In anti-climactic terms, she was a perfect substitute for a wife and home-maker. She stocked the larder that was now ours, she tilled our garden and planted seeds of vegetables and flowers. One day she painted the outsides of our windows, on another she washed my shirts and underwear, and she ironed my suit and polished my shoes.

She lit up my life. She swapped the discord in me for the harmony of her easy laughter. She was nature's angel who, at least temporarily, untangled the web I had woven for myself. Her appetite for food, all her appetites, were so healthy and straightforward, and her sleep was so deep and untroubled, that my dyspepsia and insomnia were put to shame. She was the opposite extreme from Carol in most ways, especially as regards intimacy. She showed her beautiful body without self-consciousness or ulterior motives – she had no more false modesty than an animal. The saying that we were as one might be applied to us, except for my having another self that she did not know, who had twice attempted to buy the love of my ex-wife by acts of betrayal.

After we had been together for about a week she announced at breakfast that she had to go to University Y.

My chin must have dropped or something.

She laughingly reassured me: 'I've got to do research in its library.'

What research, which of several libraries, I wondered, I regretted, having assumed she was working for me rather than for herself while we were together – or else that I was a sort of holiday for her.

'Don't worry,' she said, 'I may see Clem and Viad by accident, but I won't invite them over. And I may be late back this evening.'

'It's a long bicycle ride,' I warned.

'I've done longer,' she laughed, and then it was kisses and waves goodbye again.

Second or third thought for me was that she had gone for good. I was desperate enough to go and look for her saddle-bag and check that her clothes were in place. I even entertained a mad idea of confiscating her passport, and hunted for it high and low.

Failure to find it meant that she could have run away to another country. On the other hand everything else told a different story – she had even prepared vegetables for our supper. She must have her passport in her bag or a pocket, I deduced – and then upset myself with the next question, why she was carrying it around in the depths of a country of which I had presumed she was a citizen.

Reunion spelt relief. It obliterated the

need for answers to awkward questions. She seemed to be as overjoyed as I was, and our larynxes as well as the other parts of our anatomies celebrated our love. We could scarcely stop talking to each other, maybe we both feared we might not have time to complete the conversation.

It was not all love's nothings. That day or the next she spoke of her childhood, which had been more moneyed than mine, and I revealed the humbleness of Gladstone Road in Thornwick. We again skated successfully over thin ice, other loves, for instance, and how she had arrived at a Portuguese university. She was intrigued by my accounts of colleagues at Camp X, the unworldliness of some, their inability to catch a train although they were able to plot a voyage to a distant star, and the difficulties others had with money, paying for things with it, and not losing it.

Arthur, his views and peculiarities, fascinated her. I had disclosed that his name for the dark lady in my life was 'the thunderbolt', because she had apparently dropped out of the sky: sometimes she would try to imitate thunder to make me laugh. She was amused by Arthur's fads, the wooden Japanese pillow he slept on, and his notion that he must eat fish, although he hated it, in order to fuel his grey cells. She objected to his doctrine of self-sufficiency – 'friends are time-wasters ... social life is for dimwits' – while admiring the successes of his workaholic schedule: I had mentioned two or three of the publicly recorded high points of his career.

She was intrigued by the geography of Camp X and where and how we worked there. I described the bed-sitting rooms or bed-workrooms, a few with laboratories attached; the cell-like offices, one of which had become mine after I moved into the cottage; the conference rooms and the canteen offering sustenance of some kind on a twenty-four hour basis. Yes, everything possible was done to further the exploratory output of the theorists who had supplied government with advantageous information during the 'hot' war, and were continuing to do so in the Cold War between the West and the USSR.

Sometimes Erica and I talked politics – not in a way that worried me.

Her departure was sudden. Between mouthfuls of breakfast she said she was buzzing off for a bit, and we were kissing each other goodbye before I went to work.

'Do you have to?' I asked yet again.

'I'll be back soon,' she replied.

She was sitting on her bike when she asked me: 'Would you do me a favour, Alan?'

'Of course – if I can.'

'Not now – one day – and not for me – for the good of the cause – would you borrow a page or two of your Arthur's scribbles?'

'Oh no!' I exclaimed spontaneously, without thinking, more as if I was dodging a blow.

'Forget it,' she said, smiling and looking dashed, disappointed, at the same time. 'Forget it,' she called out over her shoulder, standing up on her pedals to bicycle away from me. 'Goodbye, Al!'

How I wished she had not asked me! How I wished she had not left me! I was angry with her and wretched without her. I was proud of my negative and glad that I had voiced it at once. But in time, from amongst the mixture of my speculations and conclusions, one stood out from all the others. I associated her lengthening absence with my no, and wished I had not been so hasty.

I blamed Clem and Vlad. They had used Erica as their cat's paw. When had the three of them hatched their plan? And whose side was she on, theirs or mine? Oh yes, the cause, the cause took precedence, and all that stuff and nonsense; but, I argued, she was my cause, she took precedence over everything else, so why was I not hers, when did I stop being hers? And when did she start telling lies, and when did her kisses mimic Judas's?

In short, I strayed into the homeland of sexual victims and injured parties, of jealous conjectures, blind alleys and unrelieved misery – and cannot bear to revisit it in these pages.

Two or three months elapsed. I became convinced that I was being punished, probably permanently, for having refused at least to discuss the favour Erica had requested.

One night, late one winter's night, she tapped on the window of the cottage sitting-room where I was working. I had not heard or seen her arrival, and attributed the noise to leaves or a little bird blown by the gusty wind. She knocked again and the subsequent scene was played out as if to the sound of trumpets.

There was satisfaction of the senses. There were apologies and more promises. There were explanations – or were they excuses? We settled into our former routine, which had been the foreground of our relationship, but now, regrettably, became the background to a horrid kind of wrestling-match.

Soon, too soon, although I may exaggerate to get a weight off my mind, I broached the subject of her favour.

'Oh please,' she said. 'I told you to forget it.'

'But I want to explain. I'd do anything for you, I'd give you anything you wanted, with one exception.'

'I know,' she said.

And I felt like a worm, because I had done that favour twice for Carol and had given her the proceeds of doing it. Additionally, while hating myself for trying to convince Erica that I was a man of honour who did not stoop to theft and spying, I felt sick because I suspected her of lying too, for surely Clem and Vlad had split on me and informed her that I was susceptible to blackmail.

She returned to the charge at a later date.

She referred to Arthur and, when I had answered warily, she inquired: 'What are his politics?'

'I don't know,' I replied. 'He steers clear, I think, but if you scratched him you'd more than likely find a reactionary.'

'Would you introduce me?'

'Introduce you? What for? He doesn't

respond well to women. He'd refuse to be introduced. And he's patriotic, Erica.'

'I thought we might be able to meet on common ground.'

'Are you imagining that he'd do you favours?'

'Well, why not? Scientists used to insist that their work belonged to the international community. All this secrecy is a stupid modern development. I know lots of scientists are against it.'

'I don't believe Arthur would ever agree to benefit another country, a not very friendly country, at the expense of his own.'

'When you talk to him next, you could just ask for his opinion about secrecy and so on, couldn't you?'

'I suppose so. I'll see.'

'Thank you, Al.'

It was a misunderstanding. I had meant no, certainly not, never, but had not dared to say so in case she would pedal away from me again.

She checked up some days later.

'What did Arthur say?'

'Oh, that! I haven't seen him at work. I often don't for weeks. And it's difficult, Erica. He's my friend, and he's admirable and up to a point defenceless – I can't drag him into a compromising situation.'

'Where does compromising come in? I'm not meeting him, I'm not allowed to see him. And I'm not asking for the moon. What's compromising about airing a harmless opinion? I haven't compromised you, Alan, and you've done a lot more to me and with me than air opinions. Isn't that true?'

'Yes,' I lied again, as she had.

Another piece of her propaganda occurs to me.

'You mustn't bristle, and raise your hackles, whenever I mention Arthur's name. You mustn't be afraid of my politics, which are only a little bit more hard-edged than yours. I'm not threatening you. But I agree with the policy of our leaders – privacy is a luxury we can't have or selfishly expect. Love and tears belong to the old world, and of course they're lovely and inescapable. But I still do my best to believe that we should subordinate ourselves to the state, so that one day it can make us all happier.'

I should have denied it, shouted that she was urging the end of freedom and culture, attacked her with conviction and force; I know it now, but then, even though I loved Erica and she said she loved me, and we sort of proved it over and over again, I was under pressure, forced on to the back foot, because of not doing as she pleased. I trimmed and cringed, unmanned by the idea that I was risking her wrath and in danger of desertion. Of course I should have said, 'Enough, shut up – let's go to the cinema!' But she was the one who was kissed, she had gained the ascendancy over me, as women had always done, and I let her nag and harass.

She asked me: 'Are wives allowed to visit their husbands in Camp X?'

'Occasionally.'

'Could I get in by pretending to be your wife?'

'Definitely not.'

'But I could peep into Arthur's room and photograph his work, while you talked to him in the canteen.'

'No, Erica!'

It became a game, we began to laugh at the bone of contention of Arthur, we made-believe that the issue was nothing but play. Yet I knew with increasing certainty that someone was going to have to win and the loser would be in trouble or would cause it.

The climax was melodrama, a melo-dramatic set-piece, although how much of it was rehearsed remains a moot point.

I arrived home one evening. The black

Ford station wagon was parked in front of my picket gate. I lost my temper and burst into the cottage.

Erica sat by the embers of the fire. Clem and Vlad jumped to their feet. Clem said sorry, and Vlad that they had stayed too late – they both prepared to leave. She did not move and looked wrong, unsmiling, not herself.

'What's going on?' I demanded generally.

The Russians mumbled, but Erica intervened.

'My friends have told me,' she said.

'Told you what?' I asked superfluously.

'That you've helped them.'

'It was completely different.'

'You've refused to help me.'

'Oh Erica!'

Clem begged pardon and said he had thought she would have known of my services to the cause, and Vlad said something about a mistake.

'We will go,' they chorused.

'No, stay!' Erica ordered, and to me: 'Listen, Al!'

I did so. I listened to the Russians propounding their plan – they spoke in turn. They had many friends in England, including friends of Arthur, and fellow-workers in other parts of the country. A fellow-worker would ring Arthur at 11 a.m. on a particular day, and he would be called to one of the telephones downstairs at Camp X. The telephone conversation would last for ten minutes, no less, possibly more, and would give me time to enter his office and photograph five of the foolscap pages which he stacked on the left-hand side of his desk. The photography was foolproof and would take two or three minutes – five pages of his pencilled notes would indicate the direction of his research. Afterwards the camera could be deposited at a prearranged collection point – and no one, not even Arthur, would be any the wiser.

'I won't do it,' I said.

'You don't love me,' Erica accused mournfully.

'For God's sake,' I protested, meaning that I did love her and she knew it.

'Not like you loved Carol...'

'That's not true, it's completely untrue!'

The Russians tightened the screw. Clem informed me with his brow sympathetically wrinkled: 'Our friend, who has been so appreciative of your assistance, is depending on you – that is the problem. Unfortunately, he is an important man and lives abroad, and we cannot guarantee his discretion.'

Vlad twisted the screw as far as it needed to go.

'Our friend is not always discreet, you understand.'

'Blackmail's a crime in my country,' I huffed and puffed.

Erica said: 'Don't be stupid, Al.'

Clem held out his hand for me to shake.

'I am so sorry,' he said.

I shook neither his hand nor the hand of Vlad, despite the latter's request for forgiveness.

They left us alone.

Erica said: 'I swear I didn't organise all that.'

Offences

It was not difficult, they had said. No – not difficult, except that I dropped one of Arthur's five pages and had no time to retrieve it. Not difficult except for the additional nails it hammered into the coffin of my soul.

They paid me five hundred pounds – a

small carrot, a carrot commensurate with the size of the stick. Admittedly, there was the possibility that I would win or retain the hand of Erica by doing the deed, but the alternative was certain and carried more weight: that if I did not do it, communists here or there would bring my offences to the notice of the authorities. I would have liked to think I was motivated exclusively by love; but the driving force was fear.

No excuses!

I remind myself, whether or not anyone else would consider it an extenuating factor, that I was not what I seemed to have become, a political extremist, a career criminal, and that no one was ever more at sea than I was in all the ambiguity, perfidy, thieving, law-breaking, and threats of peril too dire to dwell upon.

What went wrong in Arthur's office was that the page dropped out of my shaky hand and slid across the linoleum on the floor and under his desk, and I panicked.

Arthur returned from talking on the telephone downstairs, and a few minutes later was asking me questions.

What had happened to his papers? No, the page had not been blown by a breeze or a draught, it had lain under three other pages, obviously some person had moved it – did I not agree? Had I heard anybody prowling about or running away?

Arthur was more roused and irate than I had seen him or had expected him to be. He summoned the security people, who also asked me questions. I said I was shaken to think of an intruder at such close quarters, and after an hour or so escaped by saying my girlfriend was cooking me lunch and promising to return immediately after I had eaten it. I bicycled home by way of the wood where I could get rid of the camera and leave it for collection by Clem and Vlad.

Erica comforted me, called me a hero, her hero, and gave me not food – she offered food in vain – but a pill of hers meant to alleviate the pangs of morning sickness.

At Camp X the consequences were a new security officer and more stringent security precautions.

Nothing so clear-cut and final occurred between Erica and me.

Her gratitude and approval seemed at first to be an adequate reward. Sometimes I half-wondered if she was overdoing the adoration and the compliance with my every wish and whim. Sometimes, at the best times, I thought I would have done more, slit a throat or detonated a bomb, in order to have that beautiful girl repeatedly offering me her all, her body, her service, her praise, heart and wholeheartedness.

She not only soothed and calmed me down, she introduced her sense of proportion into the drama. For her, my action was an adventure. She was girlishly excited, as if by a game of French and English in up-to-date terms: together we had stolen a capitalist flag for the communist side. The effects of Arthur's work on the Cold War or the arms race would be minimal at most, she declared confidently; and she quoted the saying that it would all be the same in a hundred years.

But euphoria is temporary, and ours was. Action and talk of action deteriorated into analysis: we looked backwards, or I did. We seemed to reach an understanding – partial, unspoken – that we had pushed ourselves and each other beyond the bounds of our natures. The same apparently applied to our love affair – Erica sorry that she had asked so much of me, and I sorry that I had not done her the favour at once and willingly, instead of under compulsion.

That spoilsport, guilt, gained ground in the revised accounts of our time together.

Erica's high spirits were lowered perhaps by the realisation that her political commitment had not been good for me, quite the contrary. My depression was deepened by my failure to control her, to be a good friend to Arthur, to weigh the moral pros and cons of everything he was doing and I had done, to study the political issues thoroughly. A disturbing comparison lodged in my head: we were like children who come across an old hand-grenade on a beach and play cricket with it.

Camp X, my work there, was not a safety valve that took the steam out of our game. Big bugs from the Secret Service came from London now and again to ask me questions. Arthur's page seemed to grow ever more important in the eyes of officialdom. One day Arthur explained why, although I said I would not understand a word and begged him to save his breath.

'Any page of the calculations that I am in the process of making,' he said, 'might be of value to a competitor in the field of nuclear physics.'

He added: 'The spycatchers have had to do research themselves to discover the potential uses of mine in peace or war.'

I inquired: 'If a spy had got hold of your

calculations, would your work be of less value, would it be invalidated?'

'Not really, but someone else's would be advanced.'

Arthur's explanation, Arthur's lack of distrust of his best friend at Camp X, had side-effects on life in the cottage.

One day he was kind enough to issue a warning.

He began by asking: 'What does the thunderbolt think about the missing page?'

'Not much – we've stopped discussing it – I don't know.'

'She still lives with you?'

'Oh yes – for the time being.'

'The last man from London was taking an interest in her.'

'Oh?'

'Would she wish to answer questions?'

'She would not. Thanks so much for tipping us the wink, Arthur.'

'All these questions are tiresome.'

'Yes, they are.'

'I hope I haven't worried you.'

'No,' I lied yet again.

I passed on the news to Erica.

She laughed and said: 'Poor Al!'

It was evening. We sat down to eat at the kitchen table. Silences fell, unusual silences, unpleasant silences – I was assessing my 'poverty' and resenting it. At some stage she offered me a penny for my thoughts.

'Where are Clem and Vlad?' I asked.

'Abroad, back in Portugal, not here.'

'That's something,' I said, meaning I was glad they were not about to crawl out of the woodwork and do more damage. 'But how do you know where they are? Are you always in touch with them?'

'No cross-questioning, Al! Do stop worrying.'

Her advice was counterproductive. An hour or two passed. I joined her in our bed and she gave me not kisses but notice.

'I'll leave early tomorrow morning. It's time. You'll be safer without me. You'll be better on your own.'

I lost my temper and my head. My fears and regrets burst out of me and over her like a black tide, a flood of detritus. I said she did not know what love was. I said she was a politician, not a woman. I accused her of heartlessness, selfishness, unkindness and God knows what else. At last my festering suspicion leaked its poison: I was nothing more to her than an assignment – she had been ordered by some tinpot official to wade into my life, seduce me, use me to steal my friend's secrets, and when her job was done to clear out and move on, to find another fool willing to ruin his life for her blue eyes and sexual know-how.

She hit back. Denials alternated with jeers at my self-pity. We scratched and wounded each other for hours. Tears flowed in the end, our tears mingled, and exhaustion rather than reconciliation took over. Somehow or other, at three or four in the morning, we fell asleep.

I woke to the horrible recollection of our row. She was not in bed with me. She had left early, according to her schedule.

My extended period of mourning was mitigated by my resolutions to reconsider the principles and values of my youth.

I am no historian, dates do not attract me, so I shall write only that I was in my thirties and felt bad.

Defeatism was my attitude to love. I had had an unconsummated marriage, then the love of my life had turned sour in a few hours after lasting on and off for two years. I was trying to do without sex – sublimation was a new ideal – work would have to suffice – work and an occasional night in London.

Camp X in so-called peacetime had

become a think-tank funded by public-private money, by government and industry. The secret services oversaw and enforced security even stricter than had been the case in the years of the war. The USSR had not yet renounced its prickly policies.

Arthur had emigrated to the USA: the British establishment had failed yet again to spot and encourage a winner. A distinguished newcomer became my friend, a mathematician of Polish origins, the son of refugees who had arrived in Scotland in 1938. I shall call him Slo – the three letters form part of his unpronounceable and unspellable Christian name, do not reveal his identity, and have ironic value, since he was quick-wittedness personified. He had been educated in Scotland, spoke perfect English with a slightly Scottish accent, and was a dignified gentleman of the Northern European type, blond with regular features and deceptively mild blue eyes.

We talked politics and religion. Peace had stoked the fire in the bellies of the armchair politicians at Camp X. The majority of my colleagues leant more or less to the left, towards atheism, republicanism, egalitarianism, all the other isms, and, in a nutshell, the politics of *Animal Farm*. Slo was a refreshing influence in that he was an out-and-out unquestioning Roman Catholic and true blue reactionary, and not afraid to nail his colours to the mast.

He won me over on the day he arrived. He introduced himself, shook my hand with grave formality, and asked where the church was.

'I'm not sure that I know,' I replied.

'You don't know?'

He was surprised and raised his eyebrows at me.

'Which church?' I asked. 'There's the church in the village.'

'Would that be the Roman Catholic church?'

'No.'

'I have to go to Mass at my church,' he said.

'Yes – I'm trying to think where it is.'

He smiled and suggested that I must be a Protestant.

'No – actually I was born a Catholic – but I've lapsed – I don't go to church these days.'

'Oh, I'm so sorry,' he said.

That was all. I directed him to the right church eventually. His unflinching frankness had impressed me, not to mention his unfashionable piety.

Soon, without hesitation, he carried his flag into the political arena. He was attacked by the forthright Marxist-Leninist-Stalinists, the socialists, labourites, liberals, do-gooders, the Doctors Pangloss, the floating voters. He was a dedicated walker, and invited me to keep him company. While we walked, he initiated me into his political philosophy and beliefs, and the world of his experience, which, relative to mine, amounted to *terra incognita.*

He startled me repeatedly, perhaps first by saying that the Bolsheviks were or would be done for, and the USSR was bound to suffer divine vengeance for shooting the anointed Tsar of Russia and his family in a cellar.

'Killing a king is the worst of political mistakes,' he said. 'Remember Cromwell, remember France's punishment – Napoleon and the millions of Frenchmen killed on his battlefields – remember Shakespeare's *Hamlet* and *Macbeth*, remember ancient history.'

Slo elaborated on that theme.

'The USSR is a slaughterhouse. Communists in the West know or decide to know nothing of what has happened and is still happening in the Russia that used to be a successful country.'

He detailed some of the facts which today are common knowledge, the bloodlust of

120

Bolshevism, the corruption, the internal repression, the terror and the gulags.

He made me feel increasingly shifty by saying: 'Communists in the West who are governed democratically pretend to be serious people, but they are hypocrites who are pleased to be contrary, they're spoilt children of all ages who don't know how lucky they are. Nobody benefits from communism in power, no one except the boss, the big chief, and those who are prepared to do his dirty work. The class that communism promises to help is the class that provides most of its victims.'

Slo sometimes scolded me for my lack of interest in politics: he was wrong, but I did not correct him.

He was not merely an opposer, a destructive critic, he also put forward positive views.

'My philosophy derives from nature,' he said. 'Naturally, there are two classes of persons, the strong and the weak. The strong survive, the weak perish; but in our sophisticated democratic civilisations the weak are kept more or less alive. Thus we get governments elected by strong spirits or by the weak, the cry-babies. The former class votes for capitalism. It's capitalism that serves the purpose of nature, satisfies the hunting instinct of every living organism, gives ambition its chance, develops potential, and promotes the health of the race. But the cry-babies also vote and sometimes give power to governments that console and cosset, take money from the people who earn to give to people who cannot, do not or will not take care of themselves, that spend taxes on charity, welfare, the bad bargains of the do-gooders, and appeasement – even to the extent of appeasing would-be despots.'

Another of his homilies comes back to me.

'The theory of communism is actually for the cry-babies, although communism in practice is a bloody battle for survival. Theoretically, it is cut-price religion, it offers heaven on earth. Christianity is much more difficult – you have to live your life well and be good in order to have a chance of getting into heaven. Christianity is not against capitalism with a conscience, for only capitalism makes the money which can be used for charitable purposes – the Good Samaritan must have been a capitalist to be able to afford to provide for the casualty of a crime. Capitalism does not need to be enforced by terror and torture, by secret police and concentration camps – capitalism in principle is like sex, always popular.'

Slo was as down on his political advers-aries at Camp X as they were down on him.

He said to me: 'Karl Marx read Dickens' books to his children in the evenings – *David Copperfield* and *Great Expectations*, no doubt, which are all about the struggle to become a capitalist – while he formulated the concept of the class war, war against your superiors, a theory more destructive than any of his-tory's religions. Our colleagues are equally schizophrenic – they live in comfort and embrace the politics of discomfort. They resemble brains in bottles in a laboratory – they have severed their links with nature and with the law of consequentiality. They oppose the gentle governments of our country and wish for a terrible government that would murder them for opposing it.'

He did not convert me overnight. I was not the convertible type, but easily influ-enced. I had messed up my life owing to the influences of Carol and Erica, Clem and Vlad. But Slo swung me round so that, at least, I was pointing in the direction I had chosen to follow in my youth. And it was a relief, a pleasure insofar as I was pleased by anything, to feel myself reunited with my parents philosophically, to be thinking again of competition and self-advancement, and the possibility of ceasing to be a civil servant and of offering my wares to the highest bidder in the marketplace.

One night, in the middle of the night in my cottage, I was woken by an unaccustomed sound, a creaking tread of the stairs, the slow lift of the latch on the bedroom door. I somehow knew it was Erica despite the passage of time. She whispered my name, and I replied in the undertone of romance.

'Do you mind?' she asked.

'No.'

'Can I get into bed?'

I threw back the covers and, as she undressed, asked her: 'What's happened?'

'A spot of hue and cry – nothing for you to worry about – I'll have to leave in a few hours – but I had to find out if you still love me.'

In the glow of night through the uncurtained window she was beautiful, and then we were together under the covers.

'Oh thank you, Al, thank you for loving me. Hush! Don't talk – let's concentrate on the important things.'

Her visitation – or had it been my dream? – unsettled me completely, although, try as I might, I could not be sorry it had happened.

She had left without waking me, but in a metaphorical sense was far from gone. The major souvenirs of our love-making were a pile of upsetting questions. Hue and cry, what had she meant by that? What might have been the worry I was not to worry about? Was she on the run, and if so where did that leave me? As I was evidently at her service physically, would she imagine I was under her thumb or another portion of her anatomy in the political sense? She was the sort of person Slo disapproved of, fighting for a cause that would if it could bury her in a gulag with the minimum delay. Was I to follow her and dive head first into the political quagmire? Was she going to ask me to commit another crime for her sake? Could I withstand her disappointment and jeers at my preference for the path of the *bourgeoisie?*

Each of these questions became an argument between me and my guesses at her rallying responses and dismissive retorts.

Time passed, I forget how long, but do remember that I went for fewer walks with Slo, whose clear-headedness and blamelessness seemed to reproach me.

It was another night in my cottage, a cold wet night in autumn or winter, and lateish, half past ten or eleven o'clock. I had been working by the fire in the front room, and the knocking was on the back door. It startled and frightened me, partly because of its associations with arrest, partly because no one except Erica had ever arrived at the back of the cottage – and Erica did not knock on a door in that way. I wondered if livestock, the farmer's bullocks or his ram, had broken into my vegetable patch. I stepped into the kitchen without turning on the light, peered out, saw nobody and nothing, and jumped when the door was again knocked upon and impatiently rattled.

I called, 'Who's there?'

'An old friend,' a man replied.

'What do you want?'

'I'm Bill Hendrix.'

'Bill Hendrix,' I repeated, letting the name sink in.

'Are you Alan? You're Alan, aren't you?' he queried.

'Wait a minute!'

'For God's sake – I'm getting wet out here!'

I switched on the light and opened the door. He came in, stamping his feet in smart black shoes that were covered in mud. He wore a Jaeger camel-hair overcoat and a wide-brimmed trilby hat – smart attire in those days, though now rained on and dripping. He was recognisable, but more flashy and redder in the face. He looked a man of power who ate and drank a lot – his lips had thickened and his teeth were yellowed. He began to divest himself of his hat and coat.

'Sorry to drop in so late,' he said, but not in a sufficiently apologetic tone.

'Where have you come from?'

'I've still got my house down here. Just now I walked across the field. Your fence doesn't have a gate, and the hedge is too damn thick.'

It was typical of him to try to put me in the wrong.

'You could have come to the front door like everyone else,' I said.

He replied inconsequently: 'I left my car in the village.'

'But that's half a mile away.'

'You're telling me!'

I took charge of his wet clothes and invited him into the sitting-room.

He said: 'I won't stay long. I wanted a word in your ear. You live alone, don't you? Yes, I thought so. Clever man! Listen, I wonder if you could spare a drop to drink? I'm cold all through.'

I gave him whisky – he drank it neat and

held out the glass for a second helping.

'Why are you here, Bill?'

He spoke of the old days – exams we had taken, university life, Camp X. He spoke with a mixture of authority and charm. His eyes flickered, met mine and flickered elsewhere. He mentioned Carol – a dear girl – how good I had been to her – how kind I had been to him – he could never thank me enough for my kindness in that connection; and he gave me the news that Carol was flourishing in Texas.

He had always been a know-all: how did he know that I lived alone? I asked after Maureen and Winston. They were fine, he replied. And what was he doing now? He was in government service.

It all seemed to be beside the point. He was procrastinating, while I waited with tightening tension for him to embarrass me somehow.

'Why the mystery?' I asked. 'Why the cloak and dagger?'

He laughed uneasily.

'We all have to be careful, don't we?'

'Do we? Do you, Bill?'

He hesitated, and replied that he worked for one of the Secret Services – he vouchsafed a letter of the alphabet and a numeral.

'Should I know its speciality?'

'Counter-espionage,' he answered.

'Oh.'

'You're a friend of Erica.'

He enunciated her surname.

'What are you getting at, Bill?'

'You're Erica's friend, and she's on our black list.'

'Well–' This must be the hue and cry, I thought. 'Well – she's not here.'

'Don't bother to fib, Alan – information's my middle name – I know things others don't know – and I shouldn't be talking to you – for the record I've never set foot in your cottage.'

'What do you want with Erica?'

'She's red as hell, and she's an enemy of this country. I'm here to warn you, I'm repaying you for rescuing me from Carol.'

'I suppose I ought to thank you.'

He shrugged his shoulders and said: 'I know Erica's attractive, lots of men know that. She's also a damn clever professional. She persuades her lovers to do little services for her in return for what she does for them. It's the old old story, Alan. Take my advice – don't be loyal and gentlemanly if push comes to shove – you blame Erica as she'd blame you if it got her off the hook.'

'You astonish me, Bill. Aren't you on the wrong side? Haven't you changed sides?'

'I have not. Why say a thing like that? You're wide of the mark. I already had links with my HQ when I worked at Camp X.'

'Well – my little services – my big service, if that's what you're referring to, dates back to your mistress Carol. Carol's baby could be called my evil genius – or was that her lover and the father of the child? Why I thought you'd changed sides is because I met Clem and Vlad in your house – they were your friends before they decided to become acquaintances of mine.'

'Steady on, Alan! Let's stick to the point. These acquaintances of yours, what are their names?'

'Don't pretend you've forgotten!'

'Remind me.'

'Clemens and Vladimir – they're Russians from Portugal. They pose as academics.'

'I entertained any number of foreign academics.'

'They're Russian spies, Bill. You did me a bad turn by introducing us.'

'I'm not responsible for your activities. An introduction isn't a capital crime. Don't try to make out that I'm guilty.'

'Same to you!'

'Okay, Alan! That's not funny. You've got damn all to laugh at. I'm in charge of your case at present, for the time being, and I know enough to hang you, whereas you've no evidence to support your accusations. The state backs me, you're discredited – nobody's going to believe you. No, listen – I'll do my level best to save your bacon so long as you don't try to associate me with dodgy Russians in the distant past.'

'Are those the brass tacks? Are they why you're here?'

'I ask the questions, I don't answer them. If you keep your mouth shut, I won't open mine. Is it a deal?'

'What about Erica?'

'Erica's not my pigeon – I can't protect Erica – if Erica dupes you, I can't help it – Erica's your problem.'

'I see.'

'I hope you do for your own good. Where's my coat?'

I fetched it for him, and he asked if it was still raining.

'Why don't you go back to the village by the road?' I suggested.

'Not on your life! Honestly, Alan, you don't seem to understand the seriousness of the business you and I are in. How do I get through your hedge?'

I accompanied him into the back garden and showed him a gap. He clambered over the wire and plodded into the darkness.

'Are there cows in the fields?' he called over his shoulder.

'Not many,' I returned. 'Be brave!'

My last two words, addressed to the rear view of Bill Hendrix, were applicable to myself – I had been speaking to myself.

I was extremely alarmed and correspondingly angry. Bravery was never my strong suit: my predicament was traceable to the cowardice of feeling I was too poor to marry Carol. The paralysis of the rest of the night of Bill's visit gave way to thoughts of revenge, and deepening desires to beat, squash and crush him.

Weeks passed slowly, without the type of knock on my front door that I dreaded, but also without my finding any peace of mind.

Then Erica materialised in my bedroom again. She crept into my bed although I had not given her permission and my welcome had been curmudgeonly.

'You shouldn't be here,' I had said.

'Forgive me, I'm so cold and lonely,' she replied.

Sex was not the main event, as on the previous occasion – it was the overture. As soon as we were finished, I told her about Bill Hendrix's visit. She extracted every detail from my memory, including his charges that she was a political prostitute and would be prepared to cash me in if need be. She listened, commenting only on his character– 'Typical... How like him... Not surprising... What a bastard he is!' She brushed aside his description of her, as if it were too far-fetched to merit our attention. I remarked that she seemed to know an awful lot about Bill.

'He and his merry men are out for my blood. We've been playing cat and mouse for ages.'

'Have you met him?'

'No – but I've seen him – red-faced with greedy lips.'

I told her how angry he had made me, and that I had been allergic to him since we were boys competing for scholarships.

Erica said: 'He's a whited sepulchre.'

At my request she explained haltingly, maybe not wanting to shock me with the extent of her knowledge, that spy-catcher Bill had known Clem and Vlad much better than he had let on.

'He's done his bit for Mother Russia.'

'Are you sure?'

'Certain.'

'I suspected it. I half-accused Bill when he was here.'

'What did he say?'

'He said "Steady on".'

'We're planning to call his bluff.'

'How?'

'Obtain evidence, evidence that would keep him out of our hair – your hair as well as ours.'

'Are you talking about blackmail, more blackmail?'

'No – we'd like to uncloak him – just warn him he'd have a price to pay for putting us behind bars – and stop him interfering in our work.'

'He needs cutting down to size.'

'Exactly.'

'I'd quite like to help to cut him down.'

'Is that an offer, Al?'

'What?'

'I know you loathed that Arthur episode, I've been sad about it. Since then, I've always bitten my tongue when your assistance would have been invaluable. But, in the case of Bill Hendrix, there is something you might do for us – it's not difficult, it needs a scholar who's used to research – would you consider it?'

'You'd have to tell me more.'

'That's easy. He owns a second home. And it's got a strong room where he keeps his archive, papers, records of this and that, and, we believe, his diaries dating back for years. He tells people the diaries represent his pension, since he aims to write his memoirs and dish a lot of dirt for big bucks one day. His house is going to be burgled, and someone has to sift through his archive quickly.'

'How quickly? Research isn't quick. Isn't there a burglar alarm on his house?'

'The alarm can be disconnected. The house is left empty for days. We know his whereabouts at all times, and if and when his gardener and charlady attend to the property.'

'Who are the burglars?'

'Good people, trustworthy experts. Nobody would recognise anybody else – some would wear masks.'

'I'd need details.'

'They're not available yet. You'd receive full details in due course. You wouldn't be in any danger. And we'd be on the same side. And you'd probably be my salvation, not to mention your contribution to the cause.'

'Ah – the cause! Erica, I'm less political even than I used to be. I'm not sure I want to be of service to the USSR. I'm only thinking of putting Bill in his place, and the possibility that I could shield you.'

'Darling Al!'

'I haven't decided one way or the other.'

'Quite understood!'

'You won't harass me, will you?'

'I promise!'

That was the sum of it on the night in question. We snatched a little sleep, and Erica left me in the earliest dawn.

Light illuminated my doubts. Memory reminded me that Erica broke promises and would revert to the subject of my participation in a burglary. Logic despaired of me for almost volunteering to do something foreign to my law-abiding nature and against my will and inclinations.

I had dreaded Bill. Now I dreaded Erica in addition or perhaps even more, for I suspected that, where she led, Clem and Vlad would follow. Would I, could I, stand up to them and say no with sufficient force? Where exactly did duty lie?

It so happened that I had to visit my parents. Father had been ill, and Ethel had written to say that he could peg out. Thorn-wick, after an absence of years, looked poorer than ever, and the ill-dressed natives, the pallid children, the mean shops with faded goods on show in their grubby windows, revived my egalitarian sympathies. Was communism the answer after all? But Mother took pride in my suit of soft material, my collar, tie and polished shoes, and Father wheezed from his chair beside the kitchen range that I was already and would be still more of a credit to the family. They assumed that I was as strongly conservative as they had always been, and called me a plutocrat without a trace of criticism or irony.

Ethel was her sarcastic self. She thanked me for condescending to come home. She told me how much she did for our parents, and asked if I was minded to contribute my mite to their welfare and comfort. As a result I handed over – not to her, to Father and Mother – a larger sum of money than I had meant to or could really afford, and agreed with everyone that the politics of the left wrecked every country where it prevailed.

Dilemmas weighed me down; but the purpose of this autobiography or confession was never to plead for pity.

I record the circumstances of Slo's departure from Camp X – one of our last exchanges in particular – because I think they convey an explanatory impression of my state of mind at this juncture.

Slo had been head-hunted by a Polish university. I said how sorry I was that he was going, and he replied characteristically that he looked forward to living in and getting to know his native land, that he would be doing more interesting and better paid work, and he was not at all sorry. But he did allow that he would miss our walks and talks, and we fitted in as many as we could in the time available. With difficulty, I managed not to confide in him in full. Instead, I asked for guidance by means of questions and riddles: for instance, 'Should you be more loyal to your country or to the woman you love... What are the permissible parameters of direct action in support of a political ideal... What is duty, and where does it stop?'

No doubt, although Slo had a detached scientific mentality, and seemed to draw no personal conclusions from my concerns, he must have sensed my bewilderment and anxiety. On our last walk together, as we drew near to Camp X and our goodbyes, he launched into one of his little disquisitions surely intended to help me.

He spoke of religion, his that had been mine, and of prayer. He said the Lord's Prayer, whoever created it, and whenever created, was a supreme and universal work of art, apart from its Christian origins and significance. He said that ten words powerful enough to inspire religious people, and lead them as safely as possible through life, were to be found in the Lord's Prayer, and, so far as he knew, nowhere else.

'Ten words, Slo?' I challenged him. 'For once, you exaggerate. What's become of your scientist's pedantry?'

'You don't ask me which ten words, Alan.'

'No – well – what are they?'

'"Lead us not into temptation, but deliver us from evil".'

'Oh – yes – I grant... Thanks, Slo. Goodbye, good luck!'

We shook hands, and I hurried away, not wishing him to see the tears in my eyes.

Nemesis

I cannot remember the season of the year, but now I see all the times in question sunless, lightless, in the shades of night and the sinister tones of conspiracy.

My private life was disintegrating, whether or not with my awareness. The mortar, the bond, that had held it together was missing – I refer to truth, which I had allowed other people and events to scratch and scrape at. Clarity was replaced by obscurity, and I could no longer see my way.

Clem and Vlad came to call – I mean to call on me to do something I did not want to do. The big black car was conspicuously absent – they arrived on one of those quiet motorbikes used by certain police forces long ago. It was late, it really was a dark night, and the first I knew of my visitors was the click of the picket gate. Erica was familiar with that gate, she did not let it click; I therefore realised almost at once that she had sent along the heavy mob.

Heavy? Stylish, rather! Gently irresistible,

sympathetically brutal!

They were politeness itself. They brought two bottles of French claret – it was a reunion of partners and old friends, of good old boys who would draw the line nowhere in order to help one another. They confused me further with their benevolence.

Eventually the name of Hendrix sneaked into the conversation. He had disappointed Clem and Vlad. He had proved to be a false friend. I think they dared to use the word 'turncoat' – signifying that Bill was doing his best to betray the USSR for which he had already betrayed his native land. Bill Hendrix was bent on making a nuisance of himself, they said. Bill had a little knowledge, which was dangerous; he was acquiring power and influence in the corridors of Whitehall; and his balloon was ready for a puncture.

We laughed at the metaphor. But none of the above was a laughing matter for me. I demanded to know why I had two Russians in my sitting-room in the dead of night.

Clem said, 'Ah!' and Vlad, 'We have been with Erica.'

Between them they spoke of the burglary in euphemistic terms: it might have been an expedition to the seaside. They said they had come to check that I wished to participate in a certain important project and render assistance to their organisation and the billions of harmless and happy communists in the wider world.

I blurted out my answer.

'No go, nothing doing!'

They were perplexed by my English and my attitude.

I said my say – it was like the worm wriggling on the hook. I had changed my mind about the cause, their cause, their country. Communism in action was good for a few and terrible for everyone else. I had learned a lot belatedly, but better late than never; and I was not going to act the cat's paw for bad people in another country who were set on ruining my own.

'Poor Alan,' Clem said, and Vlad chimed in, 'Poor Erica!'

Vlad continued: 'We are so sorry, Alan, because, you see, if Bill Hendrix is permitted to expose all of us, we would not be able to protect Erica or yourself however hard we tried. None of our friends in Moscow will come forward to interfere publicly with the activities of foreign governments.'

'You can't make me work for you against my will.'

They sniggered at me.

Vlad said, 'In the USSR that is not the case,' and Clem did the explaining: 'Alan, you might be able to run away and hide in another country today, but I doubt it. And tomorrow or the day after, it will be too late – you are a man marked by Bill, who has already tried to cut a deal with you. If you displease Bill, he will catch you and put you and Erica in prison for many years. Therefore he has to be restrained – it is our duty.'

I drank more claret.

At length I asked a number of almost satirical questions, because the idea of the part I was expected to play was preposterous.

What was it that they wanted me to do? Find evidence of Bill's former links with the people he was now out to persecute? Nothing else? How was I of all people to do it? How did they propose it should be done? They said I would have to check through documentation in the Hendrix archive. The what? How on earth was I to get my hands on his private papers? And why did they imagine that he would have kept written records of secrets he divulged for gain years ago? They had inside information that every scrap of paper bearing a reference to himself, and every memorandum and souvenir, were stored in a strong-room in his second home, located not far from my cottage in which we were at present conferring. Well, how were the documents to be spirited out of his house, and where was I to check through them? They were not to be removed, and I could and would check them *in situ*.

I jeered at their impracticality; then remembered something said to me long ago by my ex-wife. Carol told me that Bill's form of narcissism was to destroy nothing whatsoever connected with himself.

In other words, Erica, Clem and Vlad could be right, evidence against Bill could exist, and a raid on his strong-room could be not merely a pipe-dream.

They filled me in, as the jargon goes. Bill Hendrix was a traditionalist, they said, he stuck to the schedule of a top office worker. He brought his family down to his house in the country for weekends. So, one midweek night, or possibly if or when he went skiing abroad, a team of professionals would break in, open the door of the strong-room, and guard me for the four or five available hours required for my research.

Discovery during those hours was a minimal risk. The house stood alone at a considerable distance from the nearest inhabited dwelling. Its burglar alarm presented no problem, and the same applied to locks on doors, including the strong-room door; and no electric light would be visible to outsiders.

As for the research, it would be particular rather than general, and was not expected to be long-drawn-out. Bill stored his old diaries, evidently, also his bank statements. He had performed useful services for Clem and Vlad on six occasions, for which he was rewarded: they could give me the dates of their meetings with him, of the transfers of material, and the precise amounts of money paid over.

The information required, Clem and Vlad were confident, would be easy to spot, provided you knew how to spot it. They realised that it would not be written in red ink: a foreign language or a code was possible, whence the necessity of having a clever worldly-wise operative to look for recorded events and suspect influxes of funds. Photographs of relevant documents would suffice in the majority of cases.

No, they said, they could think of no danger to me personally so long as I offered my fullest cooperation without demur.

I protested again. I voiced more objections

to their friends in Moscow, to their bullying bosses in the Kremlin, to the horrible history of the USSR.

They did not exactly contradict me. They listened or seemed to listen and to be weighing up my arguments. When I finished Clem shook his head as if on account of my ignorance and prejudice, and Vlad quoted the excuse of Marx or Lenin or another of the founding fathers for the fiasco of communism.

He said: 'No new life begins without screaming and blood.'

He was serious. He almost wagged a solemn finger at me. He believed he was justifying crimes more heinous than I knew about in those days, which have since come to light. He deprived me of my last illusions in respect of himself and his accomplice and his political creed. 'No new life without screaming and blood' could also have been the manifesto of the politics of Genghis Khan.

I objected as vociferously as I dared. Once more they heard me out. They did not argue, they simply issued their instructions or orders. One of them remarked that he was sure I would see sense in the end.

On the night when my assistance was

required I would be fetched by car and driven to and from Bill Hendrix's house. I would receive notice of the date and the pick-up time, and the facts on which to base my investigation would be provided as required.

They rose to leave. They overlooked my sullen mood and said goodbye with brisk bonhomie. At least I had promised them nothing.

A week or a fortnight passed – in my experience, it was survived. The nouns descriptive of my moods were terror, cowardice, bravado, indecision and paralysis. I thought of spilling the beans to the authorities, and I thought of suicide – the first could well have had the same result as the second. Eventually I decided to seek refuge at Thornwick with my parents.

A letter arrived by post – actually an envelope holding a strip of paper on which someone had written a sequence of numerals. From memory they ran thus, 18 11 23 30, and signified that I was meant to be ready and willing at 11.30 p.m. on the eighteenth of November. It was then the sixteenth, and the postman had just delivered my bit of bad news. I bicycled to work at Camp X, left early, and back at the cottage wrote a letter to my superiors pleading ill health and a crying need to get away from it all, and packed a few belongings, meaning to catch a train home early the next morning. I took one of my sleeping pills – I had obtained a few from the Camp X doctor after Clem and Vlad's visit – and went to bed and to sleep.

Erica woke me. Passionate love was excluded from this reunion. She was fully occupied with the task of allaying my suspicion, trying to persuade me that my view of revolutionary Russia was jaundiced, and playing the part of a mother having to cajole her son with toothache into the dentist's chair.

She herself was the most cogent of her political arguments. She had seduced me over and over again with her charm and vitality, and her uninhibited enthusiasm in the sexual context, not to mention her looks and athletic figure. Now it was almost the same story with her impersonation of beauty on the barricade, that stereotype which has immemorially caused men to lose their hearts and their heads.

She claimed that both the French and the Russian revolutions were inevitable and necessary, and her bright eyes filled with tears when I suggested that she could say the same about Hitler's accession to power in

Germany. She insisted that Marxism was a glorious ideal, that every Russian had rallied to the promise of a brave new world of equality and justice, and was again hurt when I reminded her of its injustice. She denied the existence of the Siberian concentration camps, the brutality of the class war, the corrupt bureaucracy, the failure of initiatives and policies, and the hardships of the populace. She appealed to me to believe in something noble and selfless, rather than in the smears of greedy capitalists clinging on to the gold they had stolen from the poor people.

We brought our argument down to earth. I said that I had been forced to connive in a felony: was that noble? I said that I was being blackmailed: were Clem and Vlad not acting selfishly, with extreme selfishness? I asked Erica why she was with me: was she motivated by affection or by Moscow? And what if something went wrong and I was put in prison for life: what would she feel, would she feel anything? I asked her if she had ever reciprocated the true love she had originally inspired, and how did she see our future together?

She rebutted my accusations with more tears, and in due course converted ideology and abstraction into the brass tacks of her personal salvation. Was I to let *her* rot in prison? Was I to punish her for being on the side of the underdogs? If Bill caught her, there would be no future for either of us, none.

Finally, sweetly, sadly, she cracked her little whip. Please would I not fail her? Please, for her sake? Politics were beside the point, Bill Hendrix was only to be warned off, the object of the exercise was to stop him doing her down, nothing else, she said.

'Please, if you love me,' she said.

I was to do it for self-interest, for my place in her heart, and because, if I did not, all my prospects looked bleak: love, freedom, security, everything.

I weakened. She celebrated.

'Oh thank you, thank you.'

'But I haven't made up my mind.'

'You have, you have really.'

'I'm scared of the whole business.'

'Is that all?'

'That's enough.'

'I'll come too.'

'What?'

'I'll hold your hand and keep you company.'

'You shouldn't, Erica – I shouldn't – we

150

shouldn't even consider it.'

'Oh "shouldn't" – how I hate that word! Listen, look, I'm here, on the spot, it's up my street, I'm an adventurous girl, and could hardly be more at risk than I am already – we'll sink or swim together!'

Roughly speaking, this was the pact arrived at an hour or two before we sat in the dark by my bedroom window and saw a large car with its sidelights on coast to a halt by the picket gate.

We climbed into the back seat. The driver and the man in the front passenger seat did not look round – we never saw their faces. The car rolled on down the incline, then stopped, the other passenger got out, opened the door I sat beside and closed it more firmly than I had, got in again, and the driver switched on headlights and engaged gears. We were on our way.

The drive to Bill Hendrix's house probably took a quarter of an hour, but it seemed an age. We were deposited in the road – a man wearing dark clothes, a cap pulled low and motorbicyclist's goggles stood on the verge, opened the door for us and indicated that we were to follow him. No one had so far shown surprise that Erica accompanied me. The car moved on, and we walked up Bill's driveway, not on the gravelled part, on the verge or lawn at one side. Erica held my hand. There must have been a moon – I managed not to stumble or fall over.

Yet another man, similarly capped and goggled, was waiting to open the front door of the house. We entered, stood in pitch darkness for a moment, the door closed behind us and a curtain in front was drawn aside, and we were in Bill's hall-cum-sitting-room, where all the lights were on. As I discovered, the entrance and the rooms we used were completely blacked out, heavy black material reminiscent of the war had been hung over windows and doors. The air was dusty and a smell of burning was noticeable. One more man greeted us – disguised like the others, youngish, well-spoken, smiling, authoritative. He said good evening, and distributed rubber gloves and led us towards Bill's study beyond the sitting-room. At the door, he ushered us past himself, and when we next looked for him he had disappeared.

The study was brightly lit, and a scene of devastation. Clearly, the strong-room, resembling a walk-in safe, had been hidden behind a section of the wall-to-wall bookshelves. That section of books on shelves, operating like a door, had been opened, an explosive charge fixed to the safe detonated, and the results were that the outer door lay in splinters on the floor, books were everywhere, although a path through them was prepared for us, and the steel door gaped wide, its locks looking like molten metal.

We walked into a chamber measuring some three metres by two, with metal shelving right and left and a desk and chairs ranged across the back wall. The former lighting was reduced to dangling wires; floodlights worked by car batteries illuminated the space. The shelves were full of files, boxes, piles of correspondence, wastepaper baskets brimming with cheque stubs, receipts, old diaries and notebooks, also other paraphernalia, a pair of binoculars, some jewellers' cases.

I despaired, not for the first time in recent days. How were we to find any particular thing in the general clutter? I wrung my hands and expressed wishes to be dead and buried. Where were the details Clem and Vlad had promised me? How was I to begin without the dates etcetera when Bill had trafficked in secrets – how were we, I kept on asking Erica. It was too much for me, I declared belatedly – I was a boffin not a burglar, a theorist not a man of action, I was more honest than she was.

We laughed at that – I had to laugh; and Erica pointed at the sheet of paper on the desk.

The requisite information was written in a foreign hand on the paper: six dates, six sums of money. Agitation notwithstanding, I was miffed that Bill Hendrix had been paid ten thousand pounds for each betrayal of his country, sixty thousand in all, whereas my highest reward was two thousand and my total receipts were less than four. No wonder Bill could afford to swagger about when he was at Camp X, and to be so hospitable – he was pocketing a cool million in modern money!

The dates on which he earned his fortune fell in a couple of wartime years, and we began to look for the appropriate diaries and the matching bank statements. With less difficulty than expected we found the diaries, pocket type – they were in order in a pile on a shelf, kept since Bill was a schoolboy. Statements were another matter: he had so many accounts, one per institution in about a dozen different banks and building societies, the Post Office and National Savings.

Some obstacles were negotiated – we seemed to hold the fate of Bill in our hands, at least his fate was probably hidden in the stack of paperwork we were transferring on to the desk; but whether or not we could extract from it the proof of wrongdoing was still doubtful.

We sat together at the desk, sifting the yellowing sheets of paper and trying to trace the first ten thousand pounds Bill was paid. Around the date given by the Russians, he opened accounts in a Scottish bank and a West Country Building Society, each with two hundred and fifty pounds, and he added five hundred to the household account he shared with his wife Maureen: these payments were apparently separate from monthly transfers of funds from the government, representing his salary, and from a firm of solicitors which must have handled his income from investments and perhaps family trusts. The thousand buckshee pounds could be suspicious, one tenth of the ten thousand that interested us, or they could not – a gift or a bet might tell an innocent story.

Erica asked a good question: 'When and how did he buy this house?'

We unearthed the title deeds and the

correspondence with a mortgage company. Eureka! He had paid seven thousand pounds deposit, and taken out a mortgage for two and a half, six weeks after his receipt of the ten thousand. And then Erica discovered a cheque stub indicating payment of one thousand pounds to a jeweller in London's West End – a present for Maureen or for another woman?

He had spent ten thousand pounds, proven; but not proven was where the ten thousand had come from – again, it could have been a bequest from an aunt, or the advance of royalties on a book, or for an article in an American learned journal, or the repayment of a debt.

We turned to payment number two. He had paid off his mortgage, bought savings certificates for himself, his wife and child, and scattered the residue of a few thousand pounds amongst his receptacles for cash – he was becoming less careful. The third ten thousand had been placed in a Northern Ireland B.S.; the fourth was divided between the English clearing banks; the fifth was invested patriotically in War Loan; and the sixth and last opened four new accounts with two thousand five hundred apiece.

All this money could have come Bill's way

legitimately. Yet I suffered a pang or two of fellow-feeling for no doubt the victim of Clem and Vlad's propensity for blackmail.

Our research had so far occupied roughly an hour. It was intriguing; I was playing a new version of the game of hide-and-seek that was my profession and life work; my nerves had been soothed by acceptance of the challenge posed by Bill Hendrix; and I scarcely noticed Erica's removal of the monetary material while I buried my head in the diaries. I heard voices in the room behind me, Erica's and a man's, but paid no attention.

On the desk in front of me were the two diaries of the years when money was allegedly paid to Bill by the Russians, plus one other, the diary of the year when Bill put Carol in the family way and palmed her off on me. It was masochistic of me to want to see what he had to say for himself about that episode, and masochism could not have asked for more painful pleasure than was offered by the three unmistakeably relevant entries. They were, first, 'Bloody fool! Bloody little fool!' – references to the mess that he and she were in; secondly, 'A fall guy?' – meaning me; and thirdly, 'A. swallowed hook line sinker' – a rude description of my offer to marry Carol.

Forgiveness of Bill, and regrets that I was unlawfully cooking up a punitive case against him, were not the guiding principles of my investigation of the other two diaries. I desired to roast him alive, and set to with renewed enthusiasm to gather combustible material.

According to entries in the earlier of the two diaries, Bill was overspent and not far from bankruptcy. He bewails his expensive tastes – 'not my fault that I was born with love of luxury'. He is dissatisfied with the 'pittance' he earns at Camp X. He applies for better paid jobs in government or industry – which government where? He writes of 'applications' in the plural – who was applying to whom for what? He prepares his *curriculum vitae* and records its postage on three occasions. I flipped through every page of the second year's diary, noticed that he was still applying for jobs, and racked my brain to remember when it was that he left Camp X to do his present work. Memory failed me, and I feared that Bill had been too clever to scribble a compromising word in a diary he was intending not to destroy.

I returned to the day in diary number two on which the Russians declared they had paid him the sixth and last sum of ten thousand pounds. The entry read: 'c.v. back. Damn and blast. Squash in lunch hour – I won. Better weather at last, good forecast. Make do and mend. Drinks 6.30, drop of the widow.'

I reinterpreted it. I achieved enlightenment. *Curriculum vitae* equalled Clem and Vlad, c.v. likewise. Every usage of the letters c and v, the six usages, fitted in with the dates supplied by the Russians. The entry that had given the game away could be rewritten thus: 'Clem and Vlad have been blackmailing and bribing me again. But over lunch I somehow extricated myself from their clutches – I squashed them. As a result the sun shone and I could see blue water ahead. Now I must draw a veil over our dealings, mend fences, play a straight bat, stick to all the rules. At six-thirty we'll celebrate.' The 'widow' was champagne, Veuve Clicquot, the widow Clicquot, which was famous and expensive.

I called to Erica. She delayed for a minute before joining me in the strong room. I asked impatiently why the delay, what had she been up to.

'Choosing how many pages of his bank statement we need,' she replied.

159

'Need for what?'

'Oh Alan!'

'But we can't pinch his papers – I thought they were only to be photographed.'

She laughed at me, she laughed and spoke in an exasperated tone of voice: 'Wake up, dearie! Stop splitting hairs. You've done a good job. The rest isn't your business.'

She was elated, as I was in spite of her exasperation. We congratulated each other, kissed and hugged to celebrate our mission accomplished – I was extremely worked up and jittery.

The masked men were summoned, the loot was collected from the strong-room, electric lights were switched off, blackout material was removed from windows and the front hall. By torchlight we trooped out and down the drive, and Erica and I were again ushered into the back seat of a car.

We held hands, but I wished she had not told me to wake up and used that belittling and even sarcastic term of endearment. Of course I should not have invoked the law while I was breaking it, but I had had other things on my mind, the things I had done largely for her sake, and felt she had wronged me.

160

We were dropped back at the cottage at three or four in the morning. I was sufficiently tired and troubled to air my grievance. She again jeered at my over-reaction to such a pinprick.

We went upstairs to bed; but I had not finished and said that I hoped she was not going to leave me dangling now she had got what she wanted from me.

It was her turn to be hurt. She argued, invoked the cause to which she was more attached than I had ever been, accused me of cruelty, and ended in tears more feminine than political.

I could not stop, I did not stop. I accused her of loving people, the masses, more than me, more than anybody except herself, and demanded to know when she planned to move to pastures greener than mine. She called me a fool for missing every point, for misunderstanding everything, and not appreciating the risks we had always run, and now more so than ever, of arrest, kidnap, torture, assassination. She explained yet again that we had burgled Bill's premises in self-defence, and that now, to save our skins, we absolutely had to part.

Who was going to kidnap us, I inquired.

She called me an idiot for not knowing the

161

value of the information we possessed and other people would fight dirty to obtain.

What people, said I.

Government agencies beyond and above the law, criminals who knew the price of every kind of goods.

She frightened without convincing me. The conclusion I jumped to was that I was about to be abandoned, and I ranted at her and begged her not to waste another moment of her precious time on the husk of a man she obviously thought I was. She denied my charges by word and by deed.

Love failed to clear the air. Bad love creates hatred. We did not cry any more, although we confessed to being utterly wretched. As dawn broke we kissed with cold lips, and she bicycled out of my life before the sun rose.

At last, too late, I did as she had told me in Bill Hendrix's house, and awoke from the prolonged nightmare of all the events leading up to my finding myself alone and aghast on that morning and on many successive days.

Do not pity me! I deserve no pity and shall sue for none. As for Erica, her face has been blurred by tears and time. I can just recall her bouncy fringe and eager comradeship as we hunted for Bill Hendrix's secrets, also the rosiness of her cheeks after amatory exertion, and how strong and capable she was. Love that is not at some time secret hardly deserves the name, and ours was all secrecy and intensity; moreover it enjoyed the romance of its impermanence. But, to tell the truth in hopes that she will never read it, she was another do-gooder, dangerously amoral, and rushing in her headstrong headlong way towards the pitfalls of her politics and ignorance.

I recovered from the illness of our parting and resolved unshakeably to have nothing more to do with Clem and Vlad ever again. A week or so after my final 'favour', I received payment in a brown envelope slid under my back door – two hundred and fifty used pound notes, nine thousand seven hundred and fifty pounds less than Bill had been paid, and an equal number of motives to desist from mad illegal escapades.

Whether or not my endeavours in his strong-room had the desired effect seems in retrospect to have passed me by. I was not afraid that I would be traced, caught, punished, or suffer any of the fates envisaged by Erica. I felt not guilty but simply sad. My strange assumption was that, because I had decided to go straight in future, my crooked history would not or could not be held against me.

This lull-like period without reference to the past or interest in the future was brought to an end by an overdue bit of good news. I received the offer of a job in America. Setting aside the munificent salary and other benefits of a capitalist kind, the USA was giving me a chance to draw a line under my disastrous adult personal life in England, and, apparently, escape from the underworld I had blundered into.

I returned to Thornwick. My parents were old now, and could not have given me advice about my career, which was outside their experience. But I had neglected them, had not seen enough of them, and wished at least to bid them a probably final farewell.

Father's face was blanched and stubbly, and shocked me. Stubble is fashionable nowadays, but was then and always will be repulsive; and it was so unlike my father, and, for that matter, my mother, to put up with it. She was thinner and greyer, but showed the same aspirational spirit. That neither he nor she reproached me for forgetting them, and that their thanks for my visit were so generous, increased my difficulties.

I told them about the American job.

Father said, 'You grab it,' and Mother, 'It'll get you out of your rut at Camp X – you'll be allowed success over there – I see you on the road to fame and fortune, which makes me happy.'

I told them I was thinking of applying for American citizenship.

Father said, 'I wouldn't blame you, the lefties have ruined our country,' and Mother, despite her concerned expression, chimed in, 'You'll be in the new world, and I suppose you'll be living a new life.'

I endorsed her opinion. I agreed with her, and mentioned my failed marriage, my entanglement with another woman, the lack of opportunities in the UK for people with my qualifications, the middle-brow or even lowbrow culture, the inverted snobbery.

'What are you saying?' Mother asked.

'I may not come back from America.'

They took it very well. We all behaved well, all except my sister Ethel. But I ignored her asides – 'Good riddance!' and 'Poor America!' – and tried to explain the inexplicable. Unfortunately I could not tell my parents that the USA looked like a safe haven and that I would not be leaving it until I was in the clear, probably long after they were dead.

My half-truths, my half-hopes of a fertile American wife, sounded lame and selfish to me. The one redeeming feature was that I made no false and unkind promises.

Mother and I had a tearful session together. I thanked her for helping me up ladders and protecting me from snakes, and she thanked me for realising her girlhood's dream of bearing a gifted child. I urged her to forgive my faults, and not to forget that I meant well. She sobbed yes, yes, and urged me one day to make my peace with God and the church. I hugged her goodbye, and for the first and last time surprised Father with a kiss on his forehead.

On the journey home to my cottage I counted the loose ends that were tidied up, and seemed to be breathing premature breaths of fresh and free air from another continent.

In the cottage, on a slip of paper pushed under the back door, somebody had written: 'Sorry – you asked for it.'

The Reckoning

Nothing happened for ten days or so. All I remember is that I was overwhelmed by disappointment and dread.

They arrived one evening. I had eaten my supper – it must have been eight-thirtyish. They arrived on a motorbike, a middle-aged grey-haired man and another, a dark young chap with curly hair. The older one wore corduroy trousers and a loose tweed jacket, the younger wore what was later called a bomber jacket, a black leather blouson with zip. The weather was mild and dry – no heavy motorbiking gear was required.

I opened the door in response to their superfluous knock – I had been waiting and watching for visitors.

'Yes?'

My voice embarrassed me – my heart seemed to be in my mouth.

'We've come for a chat.'

'Oh yes?'

'Can we come in?'

'Who are you?'

'Bill Hendrix sent us.'

'I see.'

The grey-haired man did the talking. We sat down in the front room. They offered cigarettes and lit their own, while I hunted for an ashtray.

'Nice little place,' one of them said.

'Near my work.'

'Exactly.'

'How can I help?'

'Leakage of classified information...'

'What's that?'

'That's officialese. Someone's been selling secrets – that's English.'

'Oh?'

'Would you like to tell us about it?'

'I've nothing to tell.'

'We're clued up. Maybe we should tell you. But we're all in the same business – it'd make life easier for everyone if you did the telling.'

'Sorry – there must be a misunderstanding – I used to know Bill Hendrix – but that was years ago.'

'We've lots of time. You think things over. I suppose you haven't got a drink on the premises?'

I fetched them drinks, a bottle of whisky, bottles of beer. I made them pour their own because my hands shook so much. They drank and smoked, as relaxed and sure of themselves as I was the opposite. If they had been official, policemen in uniforms taking notes, I would have been less disturbed and fearful – these men were beyond the pale of legality, brigands bound by no recognisable code, who might do me grievous harm at any moment.

'You're acquainted with a couple of dodgy Russians,' the grey-haired man stated categorically.

'I don't know. Can you describe them?'

'A fat Russian and a thin Russian answering to the names of Clem and Vlad.'

'I believe I have met them.'

'Where did you meet?'

'In Bill Hendrix's house near here in the war.'

'They're spies, they were and are spies.'

'Really? Are they still friends with Bill?'

'We're wondering what you thought of them?'

'They seemed okay.'

'Well – they've ratted on you.'

'How's that? How could they? I only met them once or twice at Bill's parties.'

'You did them a favour and they did you a favour. They gave you the money to buy this cottage. You were getting married. They gave you two grand.'

'It wasn't two million?'

'It was two thousand pounds so that you could marry a girl called Carol. That's a fact. What was the favour you did for them?'

'What do they say it was?'

'You gave them the part of your work they wanted.'

'What part would that have been?'

They knew the answer. Clem and Vlad between them had impaled me good and proper.

I said: 'If I had sold the work in question, it wouldn't have done the buyer much of a favour – it was all hypothetical.'

'Wrong, untrue, too modest of you, sir – it had practical commercial use and proved of considerable value.'

'You surprise me.'

'Here's a bigger surprise. You did the commies another favour for so little money that it smacks of a political gesture. Are you a friend of Uncle Joe?'

'Joe Stalin?'

'Himself.'

'I am not. Is my alleged link with bolshies your big surprise?'

'Not quite. What surprises us, and perhaps

you, was that you nabbed the brainchild of your friend Arthur. We wouldn't have expected you to sink to operating in the sewers.'

'I never did.'

'It was nasty to do that to a friend however nice you thought you were being to the killers in the Kremlin.'

'I deny doing any such thing.'

'Deny to your heart's content – it won't make any difference in the long run.'

'You're giving credence to spies. I've been proved guilty of nothing. You're acting on false evidence, supplied by criminals, and I demand access to my solicitor.'

'Stuff it!'

'What?'

'Save your breath.'

'I won't be bullied and blackmailed – I have rights.'

'No – you don't have rights – nobody has rights – some people have privileges. Now listen, blackmail, you say – is that what happened to you? Were you blackmailed?'

'I have nothing to admit or confess.'

'Do you know a girl called Erica?'

'Why?'

'She's not bad at blackmail. She can blackmail or bribe a man to betray his mother. She's got the lot, including a great big man-trap between her legs, as you must know since you've shared your bed with her for months.'

'How do you know that?'

'A little bird sang to us.'

'She wouldn't.'

'How do *you* know that?'

'Oh God!'

'Answer this question – Erica's a pretty piece, weren't you interested in what's between her legs?'

'I certainly won't answer questions of that kind.'

'You and Erica – or should it be Erica and you, since she's the one who misleads men? – perpetrated a burglary.'

'Not likely – I'm not that way inclined.'

'It wasn't long ago – a house not far from yours – can you still smell it?'

'Smell it?'

'Can't you get a whiff of the smell?'

'What the hell do you mean?'

'You cooked your goose that night. We can smell it and no mistake.'

'You're wide of the mark. You've been conned. You're harassing an innocent peron. Read my books, ask my colleagues!'

'We've asked enough. We know the answers. The only question unanswered is what to do with you.'

'Stop threatening me!'

'We're not threatening. We're beyond the threatening stage.'

'But you have no case against me. Those Russians won't appear in an English court of law – they're liars, professional perjurers and double-dealers – I rebut their accusations and don't intend to hold my tongue and let people like you trample over me. Please go away and leave me in peace.'

I stood up, we all stood up, and the grey-haired man volunteered a smile that reminded me of the merciless smiles of Clem.

He said: 'Afraid you're out of touch. I will agree you're innocent, innocent not to know where you happen to be. Courts of law don't figure in the world you've drifted into. We don't need evidence of the sort that policemen look and pray for on their knees. You're suspect, right? So we'll be controlling you in future. But cheer up –we don't shoot spies nowadays! Ta-ta. We'll be back. Thanks for the drinks.'

As soon as I was alone I succumbed to exhaustion. It was like dying a little – the fight went out of me, energy drained away, I could not think straight, my memory even of the recent interview faded, I was uncaring, and lay on my bed fully clothed in a comatose state for hours.

My record of that interview, my gist of what was said, may be confusing to read: the reality was mind-numbing. I had been warned. The note delivered no doubt by Bill, that *billet doux*, had driven me out of my fool's paradise with a vengeance. I was expecting a storm of some description, but I got a hurricane. Two strangers walked into my home and told me I was lucky not to be shot. They knew everything. They required no proofs of my wrongdoing. They frightened me almost to death.

I went to work at Camp X in the morning. The blood seeped back into my brain. Clem and Vlad had betrayed me. Had Erica, too? Love's wounds are not appropriate in the story of a spy, so I shall concentrate exclusively on unravelling the mystery. My accomplices had betrayed me to Bill Hendrix: why? I had thought that we were obtaining the means to prevent Bill from taking any punitive action against any of us.

A conclusion was not hard to jump to. Bill must have haggled with whoever had confronted him. His price for not acting against the Russians and Erica must have been the return of his papers and my head detached from my body. Since there had been no public announcement of Erica's arrest, and no diplomatic row about another Cold War spying scandal, presumably she and Clem and Vlad were safe enough. Moreover, since Bill had considered he could give notice that my neck would shortly be on the block, he must have known that he had nothing to fear from me although I knew he was guilty of spying for Russia, his present enemy, in the past.

Of course the Russians and Erica were more important in the spying game than I was. They or their master, the Muscovite friend, had swapped me for their impunity. I had been a rude mechanical compared with the others, a foot soldier, cannon fodder; but I was of value to Bill who could now prove to the world that I was the spy, he was not a spy, and my accusations were groundless, the lies of a blackguard and traitor, and the excusatory stuff and nonsense of a desperate criminal with his back to the wall.

My bitterness towards Erica was modified by memories of her sweetness. My rage against the treachery of Clem and Vlad was only a strong dose of the mixture as before. My hardest feelings were directed at Bill Hendrix, a two-faced scoundrel, a villain for all seasons, an errant husband and a cad who kissed girls and made them cry, disloyal, irresponsible, selfish, vicious, who had run a vendetta against me ever since I had beat him hollow in our first scholarship exam.

He had promised then to get his own back – one promise he had kept. In his diary he described me to a t – no wonder, since I was his creation, I was his and everyone else's fall guy. I was even physically aware of the sensation of falling – when and where would I land?

My residual energy spent itself in a fever of anxiety.

I rang University Y, my contacts there, in an attempt to reach Clem and Vlad. The nearest I got to them was a telephone conversation with a colleague of theirs in the Foreign Languages Faculty. They were abroad, she said, she did not know where, whether in Portugal or in Russia, and they never left forwarding addresses.

I waited, slept a lot, passed out in cat-naps and woke groaning. But I did not have to wait for long.

The motorbike stopped at my front gate at a paradoxical time, too soon and too late. Again the two men invaded my life.

Had they come to arrest me, I asked –

foolish bravado since there was no transport for a prisoner available.

No, they had come for my passport, they had forgotten to collect it the other day.

Odd that I found their amateurishness so alarming – I would have been happier with handcuffs.

I offered drinks in lieu of olive branches, and explained that I had never needed a passport and did not have one.

Actually, escape to another country had not crossed my mind – where would I have gone? – the only escapist notion I toyed with was suicide.

They accepted my offer of refreshment, whisky for the senior, beer for the youngster who drove the motorbike.

What was going to happen to me, I asked.

It depended.

'On what?'

'If you come clean.'

'I'm clean already, I've told you.'

'Well then...'

Senior shrugged his shoulders.

I said: 'Do you work for Bill Hendrix?'

'We work with him.'

'You know he's a double agent?'

'I beg your pardon?'

His question sounded like a joke.

'Bill's a double agent. He was a spy for Russia before he became a spy-catcher for the UK.'

'Interesting.'

'I'm serious.

'Aren't we all?'

'But I've known Bill for years longer than you have. I know him better than your people in London have known him. We weren't at school together, but we sat for the same scholarships. He had an affair with my ex-wife before I married her.'

They misinterpreted my claims. I grew more excited and talked too much. At some stage Senior remarked ironically, 'Having the same woman must have made you friends for life,' and Junior, after deducing from my ramblings that I envied Bill's worldly sucess, suggested, 'If he always pipped you for top jobs, you're bound to be against him.'

Eventually I blundered into no man's land in order to impress them.

'Bill Hendrix coined money by selling secrets, he pocketed sixty thousand quid.'

'Tell me another.'

'It's true.'

'Exactly sixty, no more?'

'I swear that he did.'

'Do you have proof?'

I hesitated.

'What?'

'Can you prove it?'

'I know what I'm talking about.'

'How did you come by this information?'

'I can't reveal my sources.'

'Grow up, sir, if you'll pardon the expression.'

'Bill Hendrix was a spy for the USSR, and may still be.'

'Did you find his make-up kit in the safe you burgled in his country house?'

'What? No!'

'What did you find in that safe?'

'I didn't find anything, I wasn't there.'

'Other people have said you were.'

'They're liars.'

'So everybody's a liar except for you?'

'I was talking about Bill Hendrix.'

'And I put it to you that you're lying.'

'Not so, not so – I swear...'

'Yes?'

'I've no more to say at present.'

'Very wise, sir. It's my turn to do the talking. When we were here last time, you defended yourself by saying our word against yours. Not a bad wheeze – deny everything – and a popular one! Now you're doing the accusing, you're accusing Bill, and I think we're entitled, you've entitled us, to say it's your word against his. And your word's not worth a lot, since we have witnesses of your treasonable activities, reliable witnesses and many of them. Sorry and all that – but I warned in the first instance that you haven't a leg to stand on, your defence is null and void in our circle, and I'm again warning you that smearing Bill will do you no good and harm galore. I'd keep mum, if I were you – don't pull the beard of the judge and put your tongue out at the jury. What'll happen to you will happen – fatalism's the ticket in our line of work, ours and yours. Thanks for the drinks.'

I did not know what to expect, and the unexpected happened.

A day or two later I went to work as usual. I drove, had a car by now, a Morris Minor, and approached Camp X by the drive that wound right-handed to the car park. Other cars, strange cars were parked all over the place, in the driveway, under the trees, on the verge, in the forecourt, and about fifty men with and without cameras crowded round the front door.

I passed by slowly, trying not to run anybody over, parked and entered the building by the back door. Our doorman, Geoff, instead of greeting me, picked up his telephone and said to someone on the end of the line, 'He's here.' I asked him what on earth was going on and he replied in an unfriendly manner, 'You'll see.'

I headed along the passage towards the staircase hall and met our chief, who was hurrying towards me, tabloid newspaper in hand.

'Alan, Alan,' he exclaimed dramatically, and hustled me into our stationery store, an empty room, a pantry or something when the house was owned and occupied by a family and its servants.

He thrust the newspaper at me, and I read the banner headline: 'Top Spy Unmasked!'

'Is this true, Alan?' he demanded.

I stammered a negative.

'Will you sue?'

'I don't know.'

'Is some of it true?'

'I don't know if I'll sue.'

'Oh Alan, how could you do such a thing to Arthur?'

'Please – give me time!'

'There's no time – you'll have to talk to that mob of journalists – it's your pigeon.'

'I've nothing to say.'

'You can tell them that.'

'No – I can't.'

'Come along – you must – I'll stand by you – I will not have my people here subjected to the intrusion and distraction!'

'What am I to say?'

'Get them to clear off – say you'll issue a statement tomorrow – who's your solicitor? Say you'll be issuing a statement at eleven a.m. tomorrow from in front of your solicitor's offices, and meanwhile they must cease to trespass on private property. You can tell them I've called the police to come and reinforce our security staff.'

He armed me to the front door and opened it.

Bob and Les, our security men, were clearing a space for us to stand, and the cameras were flashing blindingly, and questions were being yelled at me, and a microphone thrust in my direction connected with my lips and made them bleed.

It took Bob five minutes to obtain sufficient silence for me to convey my message, shouting it to disguise the trembling of my voice. We then withdrew indoors, as Bob bellowed that the police were arriving and would press charges for trespass.

My chief accompanied me to my office.

Two friends of mine were chatting in the first floor corridor: they saw me and took refuge in their offices, closing doors. I closed my door, too – I did not want others to hear what was likely to follow.

'Alan, you can't fight these allegations, if you are going to fight them, from Camp X.'

I said he was right.

'I'm sorry to have to ask you to clear your desk forthwith.'

I said I would do so.

'I won't ask questions – you'll be answering them for goodness knows how long – but perhaps you'd like to offer me some explanation.'

'I'd like to apologise,' I replied.

'Thank you. No explanation?'

'It's not what the newspaper claims. It wasn't like that at all. The story's too long to tell. I never turned against my country. Never!'

'But you're a clever man–'

'Incorrect! I'm a fool, I've wasted my substance, I've squandered a fortune.'

'A fortune in money? I didn't know–'

'A fortune in luck.'

'Ah yes! At least you've done good work.'

'Not what I might have done.'

'Who knows? Goodbye, Alan.'

We did not shake hands.

I rang down to Housekeeping and requested black bags. I filled the bags with my writings, books, pens, pencils, stock of paper and typewriter – it was before the Age of IT. I rang Security eventually and heard that the journalists had gone and the police were still around. I crept out of Camp X, and bribed Les in Security to carry one of the black bags to my car.

A shopping spree came next. I had the presence of mind to stock up with food, and to buy locks and padlocks, half a dozen squalid paperbacks, and a flat cap and sun glasses. Four journalists had reached my cottage before me – two were in the front garden, two round at the back. I refused to speak to them, shouldered them aside while I unloaded the car, and locked myself in. For an hour or so I fixed the extra locks on doors and window frames, and finally collapsed on my bed with cotton wool in my ears to deaden the sound of journalists' pleas and threats.

Who had done it to me? More accurately, who had done for me? It must have been either the Secret Service, ours with Bill Hendrix in control, or theirs, represented by Clem, Vlad and Erica. A possible motive was that as a result of the publicity I could never be tried, since a fair unprejudiced trial was out of the question.

At some stage I looked in the bathroom cupboard and was angrier than ever with myself for having an inadequate supply of aspirins.

In the course of the afternoon the telephone rang four or five times. I longed to get it disconnected, but lacked the energy. Besides, although I could hardly bear to think of it, I realised I would have to speak to my parents sooner or later – it would have been preferable but too cowardly to write.

In the evening the telephone rang without ceasing. It rang for much longer than the calls earlier in the day, a quarter of an hour, twenty minutes, and at last I struggled downstairs to take the instrument off the hook. When I lifted the receiver I heard an American voice repeating my name.

'Yes?' I said, collapsing in a chair.

The speaker asked if I could hear him.

'Yes,' I replied.

He identified himself, and continued: 'Sir, in consequence of news reports reaching us we regret to inform you that we are withdrawing our offer of employment.'

'Yes,' I said.

'Sir, are you hearing me?'

'Yes.'

'We will be confirming the withdrawal in print.'

'Yes.'

'There will be no cancellation fee payable. Do you understand?'

'Yes.'

I rang Thornwick twenty-four hours later, at six the next day.

Ethel answered the telephone as ill luck would have it.

'You've got a nerve,' she began.

'Is Mother there?'

'She's at the hospital.'

'Is she ill?'

'She's ill on account of you. But she isn't stopping there. She's there for Father.'

'What's wrong with him?'

'Ask yourself that!'

'Shut up, Ethel, and answer my question.'

'He had a stroke yesterday after he read the paper.'

'Is he bad?'

'He's dying, if that's what you mean – he isn't bad, you're the bad one. You've shamed our family. We'll have to leave Thornwick. I'd kill you if I got the chance.'

'When is Father expected to die?'

'Tonight or tomorrow. I'll be at the hospital when Mother leaves. My family's having to do without me thanks to you.'

'I can't come and see Father, I can't leave here at present.'

'Don't you even think of coming... Oh, here's Mother now.'

During the pause I could hear them conferring, and was afraid Mother would refuse to speak to me. But I heard her crying and eventually she was on the line.

'Alan...' she sobbed.

'I'm so sorry, Mother, I'm so sorry about Father, I beg you to forgive me, forgive me one day.'

'He wants to talk to you.'

'Does he? When does he want to talk?'

'He can from the hospital. He's terribly upset. They say he can't last. Ethel could fix it up when she's with him.'

'I won't disconnect my phone until he's rung.'

'What's that?'

'Tell Ethel to ring as soon as she's at the hospital – I'll wait for the call.'

'Are you going somewhere, Alan?'

'No. It's not that. I can't explain. I don't know.'

'You weren't wicked, Alan – I can't

187

understand how or why.'

'I'll try to write to explain.'

'Oh well – I won't stop loving you – how could I? But I wish ... I do wish... All our hopes, Alan...'

'Sorry, Mother.'

'Thank you for ringing – it was brave.'

'Goodbye.'

'Goodbye.'

Half an hour later the call from Ethel came through.

'Here's Father,' she said.

After three or four minutes he whispered, 'Curse you!' And a minute later Ethel rang off.

Roughly five hours passed. I drank whisky and felt sick, and tried to screw my courage to the point of cutting my wrists.

At one or two in the morning I heard the sound of a motorbike. The journalists had disappeared. There was normally no traffic at night in the lane. I could not believe what I was guessing. But the motorbike stopped – I could see the two men in its headlight – they dismounted and walked up the garden path – and I unlocked my door.

'Not in bed yet?' the grey-haired one queried, a deflating question to put to someone who had been concentrating on killing himself.

The youngest man had another question for me: 'How's tricks?'

They seemed to have no conception of the state of mind of a person in my position – I suppose my feelings were bread and butter to them.

Senior spoke. 'A car's on its way to collect you.'

'For what?'

'You'd better pack your best stuff – only a couple of suitcases allowed.'

'Where are you taking me?'

'Wait and see, as somebody said.'

'You must tell me.'

'Must I? You mind your language. And remember, you do the waiting, we don't wait.'

'All right!'

'Where's your telephone? We don't want you broadcasting that you're being kid-napped.'

'I pulled it out of the wall – it's kaput.'

'Good. Do your packing and take no notice of us.'

'This is outrageous, disgraceful.'

'Who says so? Anything to drink?'

I packed. A car arrived. They ushered me out of doors and took charge of the keys of

189

the cottage. We shook hands, and I was driven away in the car in the company of three strangers, the driver, a second man in the front passenger seat, and a third beside me on the back seat. The latter locked the door of the car next to where I sat. He refused to answer my questions, except when I asked if they were going to kill me – he said no. We drove for about two hours and talked intermittently of the weather and sport.

We stopped beside a big dark building seemingly in open country. I was led into the building, through a couple of doors, and into a large brightly lit cheerless area, not a room, empty except for a knot of four or five men by a table. They addressed me without hostility, in fairly genial terms actually, and took my fingerprints, photographed me, instructed me to undress and checked my body for blemishes and scars. I signed my name several times, not knowing why, and the man in charge at last volunteered an explanation.

I was being exchanged for another spy who had been in prison in the USSR. My British citizenship was cancelled, and I would never be allowed to return to the UK. The money raised by the sale of my cottage would be forwarded to my next of kin, parents and one sibling, a sister. I could of course communicate with my family from wherever I was housed by the Russian authorities.

An engine started up close by, an aeroplane engine – we were on an airfield. Two men escorted me and a third carried my cases to the plane, which was small and possibly camouflaged. We took off at once, flew for several hours, and landed again in open country beside a river. We were in West Germany, I understood. My two escorts, now letting me carry my cases, accompanied me to one end of a bridge over the river and eventually, after delays in the misty dawn, to the halfway point where, in East Germany, a man in a blue overcoat and trilby hat stood between strapping soldiers in Russian military uniforms. I smiled at the man in the overcoat but he did not smile back. We changed places, and I walked away between the soldiers. It was a slick operation – not much jawjaw about it – no fond farewells – I was not in a talkative mood.

My Russian escorts drove me in a truck to a railway station. It was extremely cold and the sky, the mist, the houses, the train and the local people were all grey. I was pushed into a compartment in the train by two men in plain clothes. We spent most of that day in the compartment, the three of us. They were thugs, had no English, chatted to each other in Russian; and at intervals I was taken to the lavatory, and one or other of them would fetch tea or food. Our journey ended at five o'clock in the afternoon, and the thugs handed me over to another hopeless linguist, my final escort to my future home, a bed-sitting-room of the most basic kind in a cross between a second-rate provincial hotel and a hostel. He gave me documents, a passport and an ID card bearing photographs of me, on each of which I had to sign my new name; also a small amount of cash and what resembled a pension book. He left me alone – and I had no idea of what country I was in.

Survival

I was in a southern state of the empire of the anti-imperial people's paradise known as the USSR. It had a temperate climate, better than England's, and was located beside an inland sea. My town, the residential part of it, was beside the sea, which had no tides.

My room, my home, was not considered

mean or squalid by the natives. It measured about five metres by four, sixteen feet by twelve, had a bed, two hard chairs, a wash-basin and an electric cooking ring; and it was on the fourth of eight floors and had a window looking across roofs to the smoking chimneys of the steel works. There were twenty similar rooms on my floor, many occupied by whole families, and we had four lavatories at one end of the passage and four showers at the other end. The furnished accommodation was designed for migrant workers summoned by the industrial con-cerns, and moved on when no longer needed; and the rooms also functioned as a convenient sort of tomb in which to bury persons superfluous to requirements.

On my first evening in the accommodation I sat and counted my misfortunes for as long as nature permitted. At last I had to go out into the passage, brave the stares of the people there, and make the rude gestures indicative of my urge to relieve myself. They pointed to a glass cubicle like a telephone box, where a stout middle-aged woman wearing black sat knitting. I thought they had misunderstood me, but approached her nonetheless. She was grumpiness personi-fied, a large lumpy grumpy dumpling, but saw my point.

When I returned from queuing for the use of a lavatory, I bearded her – as I could have done literally – again. She recognised the word food, and laid aside her knitting and with me in tow waddled down the flights of stairs to the canteen on the ground floor. She collected a tray and carried it while I chose bread and a cake that looked less disgusting than some, tea and sugar. She paid for it all with my money and then sat down at a table with a grubby top, and stared across at me speechlessly while I ate. I wished she would not, longed to be alone, was alarmed and depressed by her unsolicited company. Without warning she reached out a pudgy hand and gripped and squeezed mine. It was a gesture of sympathy – her face had assumed a sympathetic expression, too. I was extremely grateful for this first touch of human kindness for many hours, and smiled my thanks. She smiled back, and, after she had led me back to the fourth floor, I was conscious of a tiny and perhaps unreasonable stir within me of courage for life.

I never knew that lady's name – Russian first names plus patronymics continue to defeat me. Her perception of my state of mind and reaction to it were typical of the

Russian character. They – Russians – are cleverer, more charitable, more religious and crueller than the Anglo-Saxon race. My comforter only reappeared in her glass box occasionally; but other women, then children, then men showed me kindness. One evening an old woman knocked on my door and offered me a bowl of cabbage soup. One day another woman asked me to teach her English. The children demanded English lessons, and I helped men who were passionate to learn and improve themselves with mathematics. We were all poor together, and I learned from them, from their patience and dignity, and gradually ceased to believe that every Russian was like Clem, Vlad, Lenin, Stalin and their henchmen.

Our apartment block, so called, was a Stalinist monstrosity, one of half a dozen in the residential part of a relatively new town, Town Z. The identical blocks, aged ten or twenty years, were already dirty grey on the outside and dingy within, and decaying everywhere, the cement rotting and the visible steel girders rusty. The colour of the town was uniformly grey, and sunshine never changed it. There was no centre, certainly no shopping centre as there were no shops to speak of: shopping was done at general stores which had little to sell and where queues, long queues, formed for the goods that were on offer, for instance bread in the mornings and pickled fish later on, or a sudden consignment of shoes. Some stores were better run than others, therefore shoppers raced this way and that across Town Z and spent hours of each day at it. The shoppers were of both sexes, for many men were unemployed; and children shopped when their fathers worked and their mothers were busy at home.

The egalitarian ideal in practice was terrifying. The poverty was extreme, although no beggars were allowed on to the streets. Clothes were threadbare, and old people's top coats were apt to be sacks; only young girls and children dared to wear clothing that was colourful or different; the generality of adults kept the lowest possible profile sartorially. No equal person was fat, let alone obese, and everyone was frightened, and skulked about with downcast eyes and without stopping to gossip or grumble in the streets. We – for I identified with the generality – were the new serfs, driven back by communism into the bondage and servitude from which the Tsar's autocracy had liberated a happier generation. We were the masses, the lumpen proletariat, and our faces were being ground in the dust.

And those who did the grinding were the *beau monde* of Town Z, the high society, the socialites and celebrities, and the oppressors. Their residences were villas up on the hills, where the smoke from the steel works did not drift, and the air was pure and the views were long across the picturesque stretch of water on which the fishermen in little boats cast their nets. They mingled socially up there, in that heaven on the hills – we could sometimes see the headlights of their cars as they drove to functions. We knew them by their cars, the gentleman in charge of the KGB in his large saloon with blacked-out windows, the leader of the equivalent of a town council in his mighty machine flying the red flag, the wife of the Managing Director of the factory in her open Alfa Romeo, and the lower orders, the pen-pushers in humble autos costing ten years of the annual income of a worker with no political status or pull.

Hope was not a common emotion in Town Z, not amongst commoners. Advancement was via politics, and politics was strictly controlled by nepotism and bribery: elections were by definition rigged, the new rich were not keen to make way for presumptuous outsiders. Other avenues to the lush pastures were by talent for art – that is, not good art which takes time and money to develop its potential, but instant cheap stuff, gaudy pictures, soupy music – or else by athleticism. The best bet for ambitious youngsters was sex, prostitution, a pretty face, a willing body, and the ability only to discriminate between a rich customer and a romantic pauper.

Town Z would have seemed to be a forcing house for rebellion, a cauldron of revolt boiling up and almost over. Where were the barrackroom lawyers, the square pegs, the trades unionists eager to spoil another industry or service, the students red in tooth and claw, the discontented intelligentsia, the feminists and the bullying representatives of charities? They were nowhere. Where they had been was an empty room, a fatherless or motherless family, a mourning parent, a cowed group of friends and relations. Snatch-squads operated at night in my block and, it followed, all over the place. Once I heard a commotion on the fourth floor and, although screams were somehow muffled, I knew an activist was going to be 'questioned', in other words sent north to the concentration camps and oblivion. And my blood ran colder the following morning, when my neighbours gathered in groups, shaking their heads and scowling, and the concierge – not my sympathizer – shouted at them to scatter, go their separate ways, disunite before they caused trouble. Stalin had died, but his gangsters in the remote provinces were disinclined to renounce the advantages of Stalinism.

The cloud of smoke that hung over Town Z, the fumes, the stinks, were rendered stifling by fear. I was visited by a representative of the KGB, a bald bureaucrat in a mackintosh, who thanked me in halting English for contributing to the cause of the freedom of the workers of the world. I would have liked to correct his speech thus: my contribution was shameful, as shameful as his own – we were both contributors to the systematic breakage of the hearts and spirits of peoples. But I dared not. I was another who did not dare. Oppression by violence, suppression by circumambient violence and modern methods, is completely effective, at least in the shorter term.

I had nothing to do in Town Z and I existed there for a long time. I visited the library, wandered in the park and on the esplanade, and wondered if I would ever

cease to be bored, would shake off my stulti-
fying inertia, learn the language properly, or
make a real friend.

A lot of vodka was consumed in Town Z. I
would have been a consumer if my pension
had allowed. Apparently, a disabling sense
of futility was not the prerogative of an ex-
spy. Although living was so hard for the
underclass, for those who had lost the class
war, my futile fellows squandered their
money on drink. But it cheered nobody up,
so far as I could see. It induced maudlin
states, and many men sat slumped on kerb-
sides and benches crying.

They moved me to a village. It was an hour's
journey by train from Town Z, and about
the size of Thornwick. Agriculture was its
reason for being – it had suffered the liqui-
dation of the kulaks, the more successful
smallholders, and survived the crackpot
collectivisation of the land. Now, its farmers
were allowed to rent enough acreage to
support a family, and there was a better
feeling in the place and amongst the people.
I was given a wooden house to live in, one
up, one down, really a shack, but pleasantly
situated amongst birch trees and with access
to cart tracks across the landscape of tilled

land and hills.

Why I was moved suddenly and without warning, I did not know for some months. But I knew better than to kick up a fuss, and had just hoped I was not being taken to a KGB cellar.

Life in my village was less grim but not easier. Food was difficult, difficult to obtain for a newcomer without much money or items for barter. There was one shop well stocked with only one thing, empty shelves. Bread was for sale twice a week in principle, also cabbages, root vegetables, fruits in season, sausages, scraps of meat and poultry, at times that led to the word spreading round and a rush and a scrum to grab some. Most of the villagers fed themselves on their own produce. Cows mooed, pigs grunted, sheep baaed, cocks crowed and ducks quacked to prove it.

I had no land and no knowledge of husbandry. For three or four weeks I felt in danger of starving. My neighbours smiled at me, but were stand-offish. One evening when the sun was setting I was talked to by a woman walking home from the allotments. She was the international image of a female Russian peasant, an immemorial stereotype, bulky, apple-cheeked, a scarf over her head, a long-handled mattock over her shoulder, carrying a basket of vegetables; and I was sitting outside my house, leaning against the trunk of a tree and facing the roadway. She called to me in a ringing voice, and I was able to follow her Russian and respond in my own fashion.

'Are you the Englishman?' she called, not flirtatiously, with curiosity.

After I replied, she said: 'You're thin.'

I laughed.

'Who's cooking your supper?'

I said I was.

'No – no – I will.' And she passed by.

I failed to grasp her meaning.

Half an hour later she returned. I was indoors. She knocked, then came in, smiled and sought my permission, and went into the kitchen and prepared the omnipresent Russian speciality, cabbage soup. We ate it or drank it together. She waved away my thanks and told me her name was Klashka. Her husband was in prison, she said, and she was going to be evicted from her house. I said I was sorry. Darkness had fallen, and she startled me by saying without preamble that she would prepare my bed. I was too taken aback to stop her, I would not have wished to repulse any kind act. Half an hour or so slipped by, and I investigated. She lay on the floor beside my bed, which she had tidied and made to look inviting. She had not undressed and had simply curled up on the floorboards.

'What are you doing, Klashka?'

'I will sleep here, if you let me.'

'You can't, you'll be so uncomfortable.'

'That doesn't matter. I'll have no home soon. I will not trouble you. I'll work for you.'

'Wouldn't you like to go home now?'

'No – my house is bad luck.'

'I see.'

'You go to bed. I will not look.'

I did as I was told. My bed consisted of three wooden boxes against the wall of the house, a thin mattress filled with some peculiar material, two blankets and a sausage-like bolster. I piled my clothes on top of the blankets and crawled under the covers. In due course I invited her to join me.

'No, your bed is your own,' she replied.

'Please share it with me.'

'Is it your order?'

'No – my pleasure.'

'Shall I undress?'

'Yes.'

'You are a good man.'

203

'Not that, not that – but lonely – and we seem to be birds of a feather.'

'What are you saying?'

'Nothing.'

It was nice, but a crush. It was natural, and afterwards I somehow slept as she did, and more soundly than I had perhaps since my youth, since before I set foot on the slippery slope.

The next day she fetched her cooking pots, two in number, and the armful of her other possessions, clothing, bedding, a bag of miscellaneous articles, and her mattock. She rearranged her housing with the village council or whoever was in charge – I was not bothered. She worked in the fields and came home to me as before, at sunset.

Our co-habitation was not temporary. I had thought, if I thought, that she was on approval, but she thought she was permanent and I did not argue the point. It was not like love, let alone marriage. She was not like Lorna Doone, but I was nothing like John Ridd. Klashka belonged to a species different from girls such as Carol and Erica. She was physically stronger than they were, also stronger than me. In a sense she was stronger mentally – she was more realistic, and surer of herself and her moral code. She was more competent within her limits, and never exploited her femininity or flirted. She was detached, remote, self-centred, and equally obliging and unselfish. I grew accustomed to her – we lived our lives together, and to some extent protected each other, and we kept each other warm at night.

Klashka educated me rather than the other way round. She provided an explanation of why I might have been moved from Town Z to the village: there was a Science Park close by, where clever people worked and I would possibly come in useful. She gave me lessons in modern Russian history. She was twenty-nine years old. An uncle of hers had been a kulak, he was considered criminally rich because he had acquired four cows, and had suffered the death penalty. Her own father had been tortured for being the kulak's brother and never recovered his health. She and her widowed mother had farmed their few acres, while her two brothers married, had children and ran their own separate smallholdings. When her mother died aged fifty-eight, Klashka married. Her husband was a fool – he was always fooling around – and he carved a turnip into a likeness of Stalin and put a candle inside and left it out at night in front of their home. Of course the police arrested him, and she had never seen or heard from him since. She said, 'God rest his soul,' indicating her assumption that he was dead as well as gone.

She described communism either as she had observed or had heard about it. In the village one day a car arrived and some men stepped out and began to ask people, 'Who are the richest ones, where are the *bourgeois?*' Nobody answered – they did not understand, but were afraid, and did not want to get anybody into trouble. At last one villager answered, he was a drunkard and weak in the head, and he pointed his finger at every person present who had refused to drink with him and listen to his rubbishy talk. Those persons were escorted from the village square to the wall surrounding the orchard of a certain Pasha, stood against it, shot, left lying there, and the death squad returned to the car and drove off.

Klashka spoke so dispassionately that I inquired: 'Was that right? Was it just?'

She replied: 'They killed twenty-two innocents. It was a great sin.'

She was religious and she worked religiously, regularly and with concentration, pride and quiet satisfaction. That I had no work caused her concern. I never knew if she knew exactly why I was in Russia, but she seemed to appreciate that my being there and having a Russian name and so on constituted a punishment; moreover I surely complained that my enforced idleness was the worst of all my tribulations. She therefore urged me to join her in the fields, and for some months I did so, and benefited from the exercise, although my heart was never in it.

From her land a house in the middle distance was visible through a grove of trees, a gentleman's residence built of stone with a verandah and outbuildings. Who lived in it, I asked her. She looked alarmed, told me not to stare at the house, and said it was the place where her father was tortured.

'What is it now?' I pursued.

'The same,' she replied.

'They're not still torturing people?'

'They are devils.'

'Do you mean secret police?'

'Please, say no more.'

My first winter in the village was snowy and hard. I was grateful to Klashka for being with me, and after all she was better to be with than Carol the untouchable and Erica whom I could not depend on and should never have imagined was dependable. The fight against the cold used up our energies, but the interminable darkness was deadly.

Easter approached, and I realised its agricultural as well as its religious significance. Klashka raised her hand out of doors to feel the increasing heat of the sun at midday on the back of it, and sharpened the blade of her mattock and fiddled with her sprouting seeds on the indoor sills of windows. There had been a church in the village, but it was burned to the ground in the Civil War and had never been rebuilt. K!ashka announced that she would be going by coach to a church service in a monastery at a considerable distance from the village.

'Is it allowed?' I asked, since the politics of the USSR was oppressively atheist.

'The monks are brave.'

'Will you be safe?'

She smiled dismissively and rephrased my question: 'Will you come with me?'

There were three coaches on Easter Day – in spite of the expense, all of us filled them full to bursting. We set off at five o'clock in the morning, and bumped and skidded along the iced snow on the roads for about three hours. At the monastery we joined queues and crowds, were given savoury bread and tea, then entered the church. It was dramatic – the large dark space, the brilliant flickering light of innumerable candles, the silver on the icons and the golden vestments of the priests. The service lasted for hours, and we stood throughout – it did not seem over-long. The scene was beautiful and moving – objectively beautiful, beautiful enough to be an opera – and the rich deep voices of the monks chanted the prayers operatically; but the even more moving part was the contrast between the faith, piety, sincerity and emotional purity of the clergy and congregation, not to mention their courage, and the world outside of materialistic dogma and decades of strife.

We emerged into sunny weather. Snow was dropping from the pitched roofs of the monastery buildings, and the golden dome of the church glowed and glinted beacon-like. Birds were singing somewhere, spring was on the way. Friends embraced one another. Klashka hugged me, and she gazed into my eyes and repeated the words on everyone's lips as if to reassure and give me new hope: 'Christ is risen'.

In the coach, standing and swaying, in the least auspicious physical circumstances, I at last looked over my shoulder, at the past, at my home and religious upbringing, at my

First Communion and the rest of it.

I looked at the past and, as some sage remarked, was therefore able to look into the future. I was activated to the extent of wondering what I ought to do and how to do it. As a result I fell foul of what might be called the Lazarus syndrome: the difficulty of having been raised from the dead.

I wrote to my mother. It was a comfort to try to tell her my secrets, my regrets. But after posting my letter I was afraid I had done another wrong thing, that it would be the opposite of a comfort to her. No reply ever reached me. Perhaps she had been distressed to know I was still alive, or disapproved of my sentiments, or had decided not to write back, or was dead: a range of bruising possibilities. Then I suspected that letters to and from England would be censored, were sure to be censored, and felt that mine had been an exercise in sentimentality and wishful thinking.

I had wished belatedly to write other letters, to Slo, my high-minded Polish friend and former colleague, and to Arthur, to apologise for stealing from him; but I realised that such communications would embarrass them and anybody else who was sticking to the straight and narrow.

Life was proving more frustrating than my kind of suspended animation had been.

Admittedly it was spring – perhaps the spring of another year. Klashka and the rest of the village were happy to find glutinous mud in place of dry snow. The days were drawing out, and she spent longer hours on her patch of land, digging and planting, making enclosures for baby chickens, and trailing home exhausted despite her strength. Although interest in my own work was beginning to revive I accompanied her to the fields and tried to help; but holding stakes while she hammered them into the ground, carting boxes of day-old chicks from point A to point B, misunderstanding her instructions and getting clucked at for my pains, and withstanding inclement weather, solved none of my problems.

A contributory factor to my frustration and restlessness was the change occurring in the political landscape. The rumours circulating in the village, and usually greeted with scepticism, were that the government of the USSR was set on reform. There would be a new freedom of expression, new roles for the police and the army, even a spot of democracy – and pigs would fly, according to my neighbours. One clever old man was saying that books had broken the will of the commissars – a likely tale, the pessimists retorted. Yet the house visible from Klashka's land, the police barracks or torture centre or whatever it was, had builders converting it into flats for families.

A consequence of these developments was that I formed a tentative plan. Before my little grey cells ceased to function, I both yearned and felt duty-bound by my vocation to try to contact my like-minded peers and to work again on a creative project. It had dawned on me that the opportunity to do so was near at hand, in the Science Park within walking distance of the village. I contemplated the presentation of myself to qualified people who would have heard of my existence and were acquainted with my endeavours and publications.

One evening I informed Klashka of my intentions.

Unexpectedly, she was more upset than I had ever seen her. She went very red in the face and then hung her head, not speaking.

What was the matter?

At length she mumbled: 'You will go away.'

'I won't – I'd walk to work – and I thought

you'd be pleased if I could get back to doing what I like to do.'

'You will leave,' she repeated.

'But Klashka, I haven't even applied for a job, I haven't got a job, I'm only discussing my plan with you – why are you against me?'

She shook her head violently.

I asked: 'Don't you want me to be happier?'

She began to shed huge tears.

'Oh Klashka, please!' I protested a trifle sharply.

'I'm pregnant,' she said.

It was awful. It was as awful as it is portrayed in millions of books and films. It was the most hackneyed of awful scenes. And the irony that Bill Hendrix and I now had something else in common reinforced the awfulness.

'You are not pleased,' she said.

'I am, but...'

'You cannot be pleased, you want to go.'

'Of course I won't go. I didn't know you were having our baby.'

'I am sorry.'

'Don't be sorry – I'll stay with you, Klashka.'

'I do not wish you to stay against your will.'

'It's not like that. I'll be happier with you.'

'I do not believe it.'

I did my best, which was not good, and inside I was saying, 'A life sentence – for ever – no escape – *finito!*'

When we had calmed down, on another day maybe, I asked how far gone she was.

'Two months, she replied.

'But I never noticed,' I said – because the baby had not hampered any of her activities.

'No,' she replied, which was the nearest she ever came to a reproach.

In time, resignedly, although I hope not with obvious resignation, I offered to marry her.

'Thank you. No, I have a husband, Guryan the fool – you remember.'

'But you think he may never come back.'

'How do we know? In Russia, such things have not been known for many years.

'Will it be difficult for you to have the child without having a husband?'

'No – women lose husbands often.'

'You won't lose me.'

'Poor man!'

As her time approached, I worried about my inadequacy and squeamishness, my cowardice, and, to a lesser extent, her safety.

She volunteered the following without any

214

prompting from me: 'The baby won't trouble you. My friend will help me on his birth day. It's summer, you can go out walking, I will give you food to take with you. Please leave all to me. I would like you not to concern yourself. Everything will be good.'

She remained perfectly composed and stoical throughout. She worked as hard as ever in the fields and at home. Her cheerfulness never faltered.

One evening, in case everything should not be good, I made a little speech in my turn.

I said: 'You have a beautiful nature, Klashka. You are the most unselfish person I have known. Forgive me for not being your equal. I admire you very much, and am grateful to you.'

It was chilly stuff, and pedantic, but in the circumstances, because of my sense of prison doors closing behind me, I could not bring myself to say more.

She gave birth to the baby at work, in an hour or two, in a shed on her friend's allotment, and the first I knew of it, of her, not him, Polya by name, was when Klashka carried her in and showed her to me.

Polya is the Russian version of Polly, as

Klashka is of Claudia. My Polly was extra-ordinarily contented – more like her mother than her father in that respect. The three of us settled down together without insuper-able difficulties. In due course I baby-sat in daytime while Klashka resumed her work in the fields, despite my often telling her that we could survive on my pension and were not entirely dependent on the fresh food she produced.

Actually, her work was becoming a bone of contention, a buried bone to date. Owing to the political changes, she was able to acquire on some sort of hire-purchase basis the fields next to her parcel of land. She was pleased to have done so, and spoke of further enlargement and higher earnings. But her pleasure was not mine, since it was turning me into still more of a drone.

My vain yearnings must have been tele-pathic. One day a car arrived in the village. A man of relative distinction, wearing glasses, came to our house. Klashka admitted him, and he spoke to me in English. I knew him by name, a Russian but an international col-league in my old days. He had been based at the Science Park, and was now gathering a team to work with him in a fine and famous city. He had been advised that I was living in the village, and would be honoured if I would agree to be a member of his team.

I refused. He tried to persuade me. The work was up my street. There would be no clash of loyalties – it was for peaceful purposes. He was sorry that he could only offer a subsistence wage. Accommodation was available and free, but limited, one room, for the time being; but he said I could visit the lady and my daughter if and when work permitted. I refused again. He gave me his card – no doubt he had seen the tears in my eyes.

When he had gone the word occurred to me: damnation. The punishment for my crimes, my sins, was damnation. And damnation by politics, even nations damned by politics, has also been the subject of these pages.

That fate relented was a coincidence. I would not presume to suggest that I was of the slightest interest to supernatural forces.

As I was consigned to one prison, Guryan was released from another. Guryan was no fool in my eyes, he was my saving grace. He was the blunt-featured type of Russian with a big grin and a childish sense of fun. Klashka brought him back one evening –

they had met in the fields – and he was tickling her and she was laughing more than she ever laughed with me. That night I slept downstairs, and the next day Klashka wanted me to contact my gentleman. I hugged her goodbye, and possibly farewell, and walked to the Science Park with my belongings in a red handkerchief. Two or three days later the fine city became my new home and my last.

In Thornwick a slang phrase deriving from seeing films from middle to middle instead of from beginning to end would describe the experience of repetition: 'This is where we came in.' The phrase is applicable to my second chance in another country. To start with I lived in a bed-sitting-room-cum-office that resembled the same in Camp X before I married Carol. The food I ate was not like Klashka's, it was reminiscent of the Camp X canteen, and even of my mother. My routine was old style, later to bed and not so early to rise as at the village. I spoke more English than Russian, and read English newspapers.

Work, too, when I had bridged the gap of my workless years, was similar. But our organisation was not a government agency, it was a limited company, a commercial enterprise. We were shareholders as well as workers, we were responsible for paying interest on the money we had borrowed to set up the business, our pay was the money we could earn, and if we could make no money we would have no company and no jobs. What a difference from Camp X!

There were twenty-four of us. We were middle-aged and had lived through terrible times. None of us had any trust – we had the opposite of trust – in politicians, in utopias peddled by governments, in idols otherwise known as cruel despots, in false religions presided over by dictators, or in bureaucracy and the unlimited red tape issued by failing states to their bureaucrats. We were grateful to the country we lived in for almost nothing but the opportunity to create an organisation independent of it, which aimed to be, intellectually at any rate, not at the mercy of any single national authority. We were neither anarchistic nor arrogant. We recognised superior powers – in the worldly context, the power of learning, of the advancement of knowledge, and of truth. We were practical idealists, and scientific scepticism was our guide.

Camp X was a bad show in comparison. I owe it a debt, am duly grateful, but write objectively. The Camp X attitude to World War Two was not praiseworthy: its political consensus was unpatriotic. Our pay was low, discipline slack, we had to provide our own incentives, and I can remember no one being sacked, except myself. Duds were tolerated, everyone got prizes, distinction was not encouraged – Camp X was a commune, not least because in those days it was almost *de rigueur* to be a communist or at least a fellow traveller.

My place of work many years on was a model of unified effort and a hive of industry. We were survivors in one way or another, and our long hours at work, our uncomfortable living conditions, our poverty at first and even our hunger goaded us towards excellence.

We succeeded modestly. We did not go under. Since then we have flourished. Now I and my dear original colleagues are near to retirement.

In the early days of our enterprise my personal life took another turn – I formed a friendship with an admirable woman who assisted me with my work. We live together to this day. She has helped me to bear my guilt for disgracing my family, and has forgiven me for selling my secrets to a vile regime that robbed her of her husband, children and brothers; and she has helped me to make peace with my church. I prefer not to tempt providence by writing any more in the context.

My heart is apt to bleed for my native land as depicted in its newspapers. How can my former compatriots elect governments that seem to be intent on tearing it apart? Communism-socialism reduced the old USSR to a shambles, inspired fascism and nazism, bedevilled the twentieth century, and has failed everywhere, yet the Great Britain of yore and other countries continue to vote to be governed by socialists and closet-communists.

I am a capitalist now, an individualist, and believe that Everyman should be free to try to become the master of his own fate – Everyman and every woman; and can at last agree with my father that debased collectivism and subservience to the state are to blame.

Perhaps Father was also right, true to his principles, to curse me.

I shall not make a tract of my story; but cannot forget Klashka's recollection of the four class warriors who visited her village once upon a time. Their mission was to get rid of people who might obstruct the reforms that they were convinced would make for greater happiness. They did not know the villagers, they had to seek advice as to who were good by their standards and who were bad. They picked as adviser a drunken wastrel; and he got twenty-two of his betters shot without trial. The episode is representative of the politics which is based on a mistake, a misunderstanding of human nature, on another quite good revolutionary intention leading to hell for millions upon millions of people, especially the 'workers of the world', the humble masses and the aspiring lower class.

In church I remember Slo and his comments on the Lord's Prayer. He said that ten words of that prayer were the potential basis of a religion. Often I have added one word to the ten, so that the sentence refers not only to me personally but also to the next century and millennium, and prayed: 'Lead us not into temptation *again,* but deliver us from evil.'

The publishers hope that this book has given you enjoyable reading. Large Print Books are especially designed to be as easy to see and hold as possible. If you wish a complete list of our books please ask at your local library or write directly to:

Dales Large Print Books
Magna House, Long Preston,
Skipton, North Yorkshire.
BD23 4ND

This Large Print Book, for people
who cannot read normal print,
is published under the auspices of

THE ULVERSCROFT FOUNDATION

... we hope you have enjoyed this book.
Please think for a moment about those
who have worse eyesight than you ...
and are unable to even read or enjoy
Large Print without great difficulty.

You can help them by sending a
donation, large or small, to:

**The Ulverscroft Foundation,
1, The Green, Bradgate Road,
Anstey, Leicestershire, LE7 7FU,
England.**
or request a copy of our brochure for
more details.

The Foundation will use all donations
to assist those people who are visually
impaired and need special attention
with medical research, diagnosis
and treatment.

Thank you very much for your help.